# Like Smo

A Josie Facundo story
by
Isaac Lind

*Headland*
PublicationS

This is a work of fiction. Similarities to real people, places, or events are entirely coincidental.

LIKE SMOKE IN THE WIND

First edition. November 12, 2022.

Copyright © 2022 Isaac Lind.

Written by Isaac Lind.

Isaac Lind. Like Smoke in the Wind

Headland Publication LLC.

# Chapter 1

"You dirty, lying rascal..."

The shouting from the main hall reached Josie Facundo in the kitchen, and she immediately knew what had happened.

"Hmm, the delightful sound of a divided small town," she said before she braced herself. It was days before the all-important annual flea market at the Salvation Army in Kayne. This was the biggest fund raiser they had through the year, and now the main hall, which usually served as a place for worship, was filled with old furniture and boxes of stuff donated to the flea market.

"Why can't you throw out your garbage like every other person rather than troubling the Army with it," Frank shouted as Josie came out of the kitchen.

"Mind you, my garbage is worth more than your mother's silver," George spat back at him.

Frank stood in front of the mercy seat, staring with malice toward George, who had just entered the hall.

"I'm sorry. I was sure George would come by later," Ernie whispered to Josie.

"It's okay," Josie replied. When Josie came to Kayne as her first appointment as an officer in the Salvation Army, she was told about the age-old quarrel between Frank and George. Her first thought was that they were two adults that could both behave. She soon learned that George and Frank never even tried to behave. The way the people of Kayne handled this was to keep them apart, something that was literally impossible in a town with three hundred inhabitants.

"Don't worry, Frank, I won't stay long. I can't stand the stench," George replied.

"George - Frank!" Josie looked hard at George and then to Frank. "This might not look like much right now, but you are still in the house of God, and you will respect that."

Frank bit his lip and looked down at the floor, and George looked away. All the people helping with the flea market were dividing into groups. Those who sided with Frank moved into the hall toward the platform where Frank stood, and those who sided with George moved over to his side of the hall. A third group, in this case, Ernie and Marge, who didn't want to side with anyone, stood in the middle crippled by fear that any action would give the impression that they sided with someone. Josie knew it was all up to her. She couldn't throw them both out, because that would cause them to fight outside. At their age, both almost in their nineties, that could give either of them a heart attack. She couldn't ask just one of them to leave, because then it would look as if she sided with the other. And, of course, they couldn't just stand there; there was too much that needed to be done.

"George, can you please step into my office," she said directly to George before she turned to Frank. "Frank, can you come to the kitchen?"

They both nodded and exchanged a hostile gaze as they moved in their assigned direction.

"Coffee and cakes, and the exact same size on each plate," she whispered to Marge. She nodded and followed Frank into the kitchen. Josie watched as George found his way into her office before she went into the kitchen.

"Frank, I can't have something like this during the flea market on Saturday."

"Come on, I always behave during the flea market. I guess there are others you need to talk to."

Josie said nothing. She just looked at him with her big brown eyes and a concerned countenance.

It took a minute before Frank took a deep breath, followed by a long exhale.

"I'm sorry, Lieutenant," he said, barely audible.

Josie's face broke into a big smile, and she gave him a hug.

"I'm not apologizing," George said as she entered the office with coffee and cake.

"I'm not asking you to either," she replied as she served him.

"You're not?"

## LIKE SMOKE IN THE WIND

"My dad used to say that you don't need to ask a reasonable man to do the reasonable thing, and there is no point in asking the unreasonable man to do it."

George gazed for a long time into his cup of coffee.

"I'm sorry," he said finally. Josie wasn't sure it was because he was reasonable or it was because he wanted to be perceived as reasonable, but she'd take it anyway.

"Thanks," she said and smiled. Her dad also used to say that the reason Josie was so spoiled was because no one could resist that wavy smile of hers. "Are we good on Saturday?"

George nodded.

When Frank and George were apart, they were both so sweet, but put together, they were everything that was wrong with Kayne. But what the old quarrel was about, no one would tell her. Everyone she asked only said that it had been so for decades. *Even a better reason to get it resolved,* Josie thought, but apparently, people in Kayne meant it was unresolvable.

George took a sip of the coffee and a deep breath.

"Anything else I can do for you?" he said.

*Not really,* Josie thought, but she couldn't let him out into the hall before Frank had left, so she needed to stall. "Well, there is one thing," she said. "In the unlikely event that we don't get to sell every item at the flea market."

George smiled. "Of course you can store all the usable stuff in my shed," he said.

"Can you ask Jerry if he will help out with the transportation as well?"

"Why not ask him yourself?" George said, mumbling, with a piece of cake in his mouth.

"The odds of a positive answer are better if you ask," she replied.

"Sure." He nodded. "Shall I ask him to take the garbage as well?"

"That would be perfect," she said and found the "to-do" list for the flea market. She had made herself a list of everything that needed to be done before, during and after the flea market. The list made her feel a lot more in control this year than she had been last year. After "storing leftovers," she wrote "George," and after "garbage," she wrote "Jerry," taking it for granted that when George asked, Jerry would say yes. "I have this cunning plan for the garbage this year. This year, more stuff will end up in the garbage than in your shed."

"That's a good plan. I believe there is stuff that has gone in and out of my shed for years without being sold."

"My plan is that nothing is going back into your shed for the second time."

"That sounds like a good plan."

In that moment, Marge entered the office. "There's more coffee in the kitchen if you'd like some."

George smiled, and Marge gave Josie a subtle nod. Josie understood it was a code for saying Frank had left, and the coast was clear. She nodded back. Disaster was avoided this time as well.

"Well, that's enough about after the flea market. Now we need to focus on the preparations," Josie said.

"About that, I brought something to sell at the market," George said.

"Find Ernie and he will know where to place them, and Josie will come and price them later," Marge said.

"Thank you for the quick thinking," Marge said as soon as they were alone in the office.

"You're welcome," Josie said. "But are we supposed to balance everything between those two for the rest of their lives?" Everything they planned, they had to think about keeping Frank and George apart. After one year at this, Josie was already fed up. In a month, her divisional commander, the leader of the Salvation Army in the northern part of the Western territory, would come visiting. She knew he would ask whether she would like to be moved or if she would stay on for another year. This conflict was about to tip her decision toward leaving.

"I'm afraid so," Marge said. "If they haven't reconciled after forty years, my guess is they won't."

Josie nodded but said nothing.

"Well, we'll have to get moving. Saturday at nine, this house will be packed."

# Chapter 2

Josie was in flea-market mode. Her brain churned on and on about cleaning dust, pricing, and sorting out old stuff. She had been in that mode for days. But today more than ever. Not only would the total population of Kayne drop by the Salvation Army, but outsiders would come as well and almost double the population for the day. As the officer at the local Salvation Army Corps, Josie would be responsible for the flea market. The past few days, she had walked around in a fog of dust, trying her best to supervise the work of sorting out all the stuff that had arrived. Now was the final stage of trying to sell it all. This was not her favorite part of the job, so she had set herself a goal, to make it to Saturday afternoon, 5:00 p.m., then she would be able to relax and breathe properly. Until then, she was in the mode: just get the work done kind of mode.

"What is this doing here?" Josie said, holding up an old rusty key. It was less than an hour in, and the silver-plated cutlery was all mixed up with the actual sterling silver cutlery. It was as she sorted out the cutlery that she found the old key, the kind used for barns and sheds.

"Doing here among the cutlery or doing here at the flea market at all?" Marge had a rather confused expression.

"Both," she replied. She had thought about what it was doing amongst the cutlery, but Marge was right, a key without the lock wasn't what she considered a sellable item. It was while she stood there holding the large key in her hand that she realized that something was wrong. But it was like her brain couldn't respond, probably due to the dust and the deafening noise throughout the hall. Then she realized the noise was gone. The hall was silent.

"Deirdre…" she heard as she turned. The hall looked like a modern rendition of John Trumbull's painting 'The Resignation of Washington.' But instead of the entire room having their eyes fixed on a confident George Washington, they were all looking at a rather confused Jack Sutton. Everyone except Jack himself. He looked straight at Josie.

"Deirdre, I have kept your secret," he continued.

"Oh, Jack," Josie said, breaking free from the odd moment. She put the key down and started toward Jack.

"I have kept your secret," he said again.

"It's me, Josie," she said and gave him a hug. Jack was not among the oldest in town, but he had dementia and his clear moments were sparse nowadays. He would remember most names, but had no chance to remember Josie's. She came to Kayne only a year ago, when Jack had already become demented. The most common names he mistook her for were former corps officers. The others always pointed out that it was only because of the uniform. She had figured that out by herself. All the female officers that had been stationed in Kayne before her were pale white and quite a bit older than Josie. The name he most frequently gave her was Major Jensen. She had seen a picture of Mrs. Jensen. She had red hair and blue eyes and was twice her size. The officer's uniform must be the only thing they had in common. Deirdre, however, was a new one.

"Come on, Jack, let's find some coffee."

Jack blinked his eyes twice as reality checked in. "Coffee, that would be nice," he replied.

She led him over to the adjacent hall where they had set up a small cafe. The noise was coming back to the hall. She turned for a brief second. The sun shone through the windows and revealed all the dust. When the hall, for a brief moment, had gone quiet, the dust had fallen down like glittering snow. But now, when people were moving again, it was once again dancing over their heads.

She found an empty table in the cafe's corner where they could sit undisturbed from the rumble in the main hall. One would think these were the tables that were occupied first. Early on during the flea market, most people were busy with bargain hunting. The ones who were in the cafe this early were the elders. They didn't come to buy but to watch what was bought. More specifically, when the stuff they had donated was bought. It had turned into a competition amongst them of who donated stuff that generated most money. An absurd competition, but at least they gave nice stuff to the flea market.

"Wait here, Jack, and I'll fetch you some coffee."

"Thanks, Major," he replied.

"It's Josie."

# LIKE SMOKE IN THE WIND

Jack nodded. Josie skipped the queue and got right behind the counter and fixed him a cup of coffee and a piece of cake. The perks of being in charge. Jack smiled at the sight of coffee; finally, something he could remember.

Josie stopped by the closest table and bent down beside Frank Meadows.

"Frank, could you keep an eye on Jack?"

"Well, I've got a lot of things to keep my eyes on right now," he said and gestured toward the hall.

"Come on, just until I get hold of Carl."

"Sure, you should fetch that scoundrel before he robs you blind."

Josie ignored the last statement and walked on. As she passed the second table, George held on to her.

"Let Carl be. I can sit with Jack."

"That's nice of you," Josie replied.

"No problem, Lieutenant," he said loud enough for everyone in the cafe to hear him. "Jack might not be himself all the time, but he still has some friends in this town." George got up and moved over to Jack's table in the corner.

"It's because you have nothing else here to look after, you cheap b..."

Josie gave Frank a stern look to remind him he still was in a house of God. Frank looked down as George triumphantly passed him. Josie shook her head and got back into the main hall.

"Lieutenant, you're needed outside." Josie had just returned to the cutlery when Ernie, the sergeant-major, called for her.

"Coming," she shouted back and waved her hand in the air to signal that she had received the message. This early in the flea market, going out was to go against the flow as more and more people pushed to get inside. It felt like ages before she finally squeezed herself out of the main door.

"Over here," Ernie shouted. He stood behind an old dresser with Peggy and Carl on each side, each with a grumpy countenance.

"What's the problem, Ernie?" she asked.

"The problem is this..." Peggy said before Josie stopped her.

"I asked Ernie to explain," Josie said calmly. The look on Peggy's face could make anyone believe Josie had insulted the Queen of England. Which was probably how Peggy viewed herself, Josie thought.

"The problem is," Ernie said, "that I sold this dresser to Carl."

"Yes, but..." Peggy objected before Josie gave her a stern look.

"Then, at the same time, Ann sold this dresser to Peggy."

"Oh, I see, and sawing it in two halves won't do?" Josie asked. The looks on Peggy and Carl suggested that even joking about it wasn't okay. "Well, then we must have an auction. The one who bids most in overprice will get it."

"An auction? Why should I bid on something I have already bought?" Carl grunted.

"Well, then I bid fifty cents," Peggy countered.

"Fifty cents? If you think you'll get my dresser for a mere fifty cents, then you are way off. I bid a dollar."

"Your dresser? We'll see about that. I bid two..."

# Chapter 3

"Twenty-five dollars..." Ernie said as he bent over and slapped both hands on his lap, retelling the story of the dresser. It was the finally-the-flea-market-is-over-coffee, with Ernie and Marge. They had sorted all the unsold items in boxes; something to keep for next year, something to throw away, and a few things to go to the thrift store in Spokane. All the other helpers had gone home. Ernie and Marge had stayed behind and counted the money, and could happily confirm that this was the best flea market ever. It was slightly better than last year's, which had been much better than the previous years'. That had been Josie's first flea market, and she was also the main reason for the rise compared to previous years. Josie had always enjoyed going to thrift stores and flea markets, and she realized that the average prices were way too low. So, by adjusting the prices, they had made way more money, albeit a few grumpy comments on the prices.

"But apart from Peggy, who ended up paying twenty-five dollars for a dresser priced at a tenner, I don't think anyone has complained much about the prices," Marge said. Josie smiled and thought about how Marge had disagreed when she raised the prices last year.

"To all the good people of Kayne," Josie said, raising her cup, and then took a good sip of her tea. That had been another frustration for the people in Kayne when she arrived a year ago. A Salvation Army officer who didn't drink coffee. The others nodded.

"Are you sure you don't want any help washing down the hall tonight?"

"Yes, I'm sure. We've done enough for one day," Josie replied. That was at least half the truth. The other half was that it was the same hot water tank for both the hall and her apartment on the second floor. Last year, they had washed the hall directly after, and as a result, there had been no hot water left when she headed upstairs. So the day she needed a shower more than any day of the year, she had no hot water. She ended up with a long, cold shower that still sent shivers down her spine when she thought about it. This year, she had insisted that they should only pack down the stuff and wash it later on. She had coined it as a concern for those who had worked so hard that day, but she realized the hot shower had been the main issue for her.

"Well, I'll stop by on Monday, and we can wash the hall then," Marge said.

"That's good of you," Josie replied.

"Jack wasn't quite himself this day," Ernie shot in before he reached out for another piece of chocolate cake. None of the soldiers had time to sit down and eat anything during opening hours, but they could dig in on the leftovers afterwards. For Ernie, that was all the reward he needed.

"No, I believe all the turmoil is too much for him. Maybe we should encourage him to stay home next year," Marge said.

"Maybe, or we should just get him to the cafe and keep him there," Josie said.

"I'm not sure he'll still live in Kayne next year. It's time to get him into one of those old people's homes," Ernie said, and leaned back in his chair and rubbed his nose.

"Do you really think you'll convince him to do that?"

"Well, he is a stubborn old man, that's for sure," he replied.

*Old man*, Josie thought and smiled. As far as she knew, Ernie was the same age as Jack.

"If he is in the retirement home in Ashville, then I'll drive and get him to the flea market," she replied.

"He would like that, a car trip with Captain Jensen," Ernie said and chuckled. Sometimes when Jack called Josie an unfamiliar name, the others followed up, calling her by that name just for fun. Josie had always frowned and told them not to help his delusions, but now she just smiled.

"By the way," she said. "Who is Deirdre?"

The same awkward silence that she had experienced during the flea market set in again. She had never experienced this before, but both Ernie and Marge sat there and pretended that they didn't hear her. Ernie, she knew, wasn't hearing that well, but she was confident that he had heard her question. And Marge, she usually had trouble making her stop talking. Now they sat there on each of their chairs and stared blankly into thin air. Or actually, thick air. All the dust from the flea market hung so thick in the air and made the lamplight blurry. They said nothing. Bringing up a new topic would be too rude, and

# LIKE SMOKE IN THE WIND

talking about this girl seemed to be out of the question. If they had only answered the question normally, Josie probably would have forgotten about it already and changed the topic to something different. But this silence made her curiosity do hula hoops inside her brain. If Josie had decided anything in the last few minutes, it was that she would learn all there was to learn about Deirdre.

"Well…" she said and broke the silence.

"Well, what?" Ernie said, faking that he hadn't heard what she said. It was probably the one good thing about going deaf. He could pretend that he didn't hear. But Josie knew he had heard.

"Deirdre," she drawled with a loud and clear voice. "Who is she?"

They both turned slightly away from her and looked down at the floor.

"Well, look at that," Marge said, and tilted her head and pointed at the floor a couple of yards in front of her. "Looks like someone spilled some coffee there."

"Seriously, who is Deirdre?" Josie repeated. She was about to get furious and wanted to pick them up and shake the words out of their mouths.

"It was George's girl," Ernie muttered, barely audible.

"Was?"

"She died," Marge said. "Long time ago."

"Deirdre Chisholm died a long time ago, well, I guess she was just a girl, and it was tragic circumstances around her death, since you are so unwilling to talk about it."

They both nodded and looked back down at the floor. The mood in the hall had turned from jolly to dismal in the blink of an eye, and Josie thought it would be easier to just leave it alone.

"Not really that young. I guess she had just turned eighteen," Marge said.

Then the pause was back on, and they sat in silence for a moment. Josie sat there, half wondering if they would shed any more light on Deirdre, or how she could get some more information on this sensitive topic.

"I guess it's time to call it a day," Ernie said, and with both hands, pushed himself up from the chair.

"Sure, and it has been such a good day too." Marge had returned to her old bright and jolly mood.

"Thank you very much for all your help today. You've been tremendous." Josie got up to greet them on their way out.

"It's been a pleasure. The fall isn't the same without the flea market, you know," Marge said.

"And." Ernie was already on his way, but turned back to Josie. "As long as our health is good, you can count on us."

"I am so grateful for that. Have a good evening."

"Thanks; the same," Ernie replied. Josie followed them with her eyes as they slowly walked over to the door. She could see that they weren't young anymore, and the first steps they used to loosen up sore limbs after a long and hard day. They would need a hot shower as well, she thought, and remembered just how much she craved the one she would have in just a moment.

"How did she die?"

Both Ernie and Marge froze out on the floor.

"We don't talk about that," Ernie said with an underlying understanding that this was the Kayne way of dealing with it and she needed to respect that.

"Listen, guys, I don't ask because I have some bizarre liking in it. I ask because I need to know." Josie strolled toward them. "I have to deal with George and Jerry every week. What if a dog bit Deirdre to death, and I talk to George about how cute dogs are? How do you think that will fly? I'd rather not wake up from those memories."

"You do anyway," Ernie mumbled at the same time that Marge said, "It was a fire."

"Wow, one at the time. Did you say a fire?"

"Yes, the old mill."

"I've heard of the old mill."

"It caught fire and the old lock jammed." Marge breathed. "Deirdre was locked inside it."

"How horrible," Josie said and almost regretted asking.

"Jack Sutton was the first one at the site. He tried for a half an hour to break the door open, and when he finally managed, it was too late."

Josie could see a sprinkle of a tear in the corner of her eye. After all these years, the tragedy still affected her.

"Thanks for sharing," she said. They just nodded. "By the way, Ernie, what did you mean by I do it already?"

"Just by being an officer. She had applied for the training college. Had she lived only a few months longer, she would have been a cadet. George has problems with officers because they all remind him of his girl that never became one."

Josie nodded but said nothing.

"And she would have been an outstanding officer. She was a lovely young girl," Marge broke in.

# Chapter 4

The red taillights of the trailer were easing from side to side like a snake, upward toward the Salvation Army hall. The trailer stopped as it came dangerously close to the corps building. Then Jerry drove forward and tried again. This was the third time he tried. They still considered the Chisholm family out-of-towners in Kayne, despite the fact that they had lived there for over fifty years. Jerry was only five when they moved here. Of course, there were things that set the Chisholms apart from the rest of the population. One of them was that they couldn't back a car with a trailer attached to it. Josie had heard this mentioned, but still, she didn't think it was half bad. But what did she know; she was an out-of-towner too. The third time was the charm, and the car got nicely parked in front of the main entrance.

"A bit unlucky with the direction," Jerry excused himself as he stepped out of the car.

"This is just perfect. How do you want the stuff?"

"Let's put the garbage in first, and then what is going in the shed afterwards." George, having let them store the remains from the flea market that they would try to sell next year, also convinced Jerry to haul the garbage away and drive the "keep stuff" to the shed.

"Sure, come on in and I'll show you what's what." Jerry followed Josie inside and she showed them the keep pile and the throw pile. The throw pile was by far the biggest. A flea market generates a lot of trash. And they had lessened the keep pile by Josie's new "one year" rule. She had realized that some items that were for sale at the flea market last year had been for sale in the previous five flea markets. The "one year" rule meant that they would keep no item for over one year. If they couldn't sell it in two flea markets, they couldn't sell it at all. Some of this had gone to the thrift store in Spokane. Still, much had ended up in the throw pile. To throw away perfectly good and usable items had not been an easy task for the soldiers. "If it's outdated in Kayne, it's outdated anywhere," Josie told them. They had been insulted, but there was no way the old soldiers

# LIKE SMOKE IN THE WIND

in Kayne could argue about the latest fashions with a young woman all the way from Los Angeles.

"Sure is a lot going to the trash this year," Jerry said, holding his hands on his hips.

"Yup."

"Okay," he said when he realized Josie had no intention of elaborating. "Let's get it out, then."

They both started picking up boxes and loaded them onto the trailer.

"Finally, the last box," Jerry said as he put the box on top of another box in the back of the trailer. He leaned toward the trailer and panted. Josie could see pearls of sweat on his forehead. It was a stupid macho thing that men had up here. Since he was a man, he should be able to carry twice as much as Josie, who was a woman. So for every box she carried, he had to carry two, not at all considering that he was more than twice her age. He was indeed stronger than Josie, but without the same stamina.

"Now I only need to get the boxes into the shed," he said and tried to sound rested and fresh as he closed the back door of the enclosed trailer. He couldn't quite pull it off.

"I can help you move the stuff into the shed," Josie said.

"There's no need. I can manage," he replied, more than an obligatory response.

"It's no problem. In fact, I insist," Josie said.

"Well then, you'd better hop in," he said with a smile, and pointed to the passenger door.

Josie got in, and the car eased down the road. The load of boxes wasn't secured, but it was a short drive and he drove carefully down the main street.

"I didn't know that you once had a sister," Josie said, testing the waters. Jerry just mumbled as a response. Just what she had anticipated. It was a topic they didn't talk about.

"I am sorry to hear what happened to her," she continued. Now he didn't even respond. They took off the main road and drove up to the Chisholms' house. This was another reason the Chisholms weren't just like the rest of the residents in Kayne. Their house was twice as large as the second biggest house in Kayne. Houses in Kayne were rather small, so the house of the Chisholms was nothing more than a large upper middle-class house everywhere else in the state. George had moved here with his family as the representative of the Spokane Valley Power Company. It was when they had built a dam and a power plant in Kayne. The car stopped in front of the house and Jerry backed the car toward the shed.

"I was curious about who it was Jack had mistaken me for during the flea market."

"Hmm," Jerry said and nodded. He stopped the car and pulled the parking brake on. It was a straight line to back up with the trailer, so he managed it in one try. They got out and opened up the trailer.

"By the way, do you know what Jack meant by her secret?"

"No, not easy to understand anything with Jack these days," Jerry said. He didn't mumble this time.

"Maybe I should wait for one of his clear moments and ask him."

Jerry just shook his head and took down the last box he placed in the hangar. Josie took one as well, and they headed for the shed. Jerry stopped outside and opened the door and searched for the lights. They had one light inside the shed, and one on the outside, giving good light for working in.

"Is it the sweet young lieutenant that's with you?"

They both turned and could see Oscar Bowers' face in the shimmer of the light Jerry just turned on. Some people had their own ability to give people the creeps when they talked, and Oscar was one of them. When a man well in his sixties is being flirty with a woman in her twenties, that was a clear no-no in Josie's book.

"I was on my way to have an afternoon coffee with Uncle George," he continued. "It sounded like you were talking to yourself, so I thought I'd check up on you."

"I'm not that old yet," Jerry replied. "Tell Dad to put on some tea for Josie as well."

*Well, that is one way to be invited in for a cup of tea,* Josie thought. But it didn't surprise her. Kayne had its own etiquette. Oscar nodded and disappeared out of the light. Jerry lifted the box and went into the shed.

"Uncle George?" Josie said as she put her box down beside Jerry's. "I didn't know you two were cousins."

She wasn't able to hide her surprise at the question. First, she really didn't think they had any relatives in Kayne. After all, they had moved to this town.

# LIKE SMOKE IN THE WIND

And if they had asked her to guess, Oscar was probably one of the last she would guess on. If one should divide people into social classes, the Chisholms and Oscar would be on each of their end of the scale.

"Sure, he's the son of my mother's sister. They lived in Seattle, but when he was a teenager, he came and lived with us for a while."

It was much faster putting the boxes into the shed. Of course, it was also fewer boxes. They left the boxes they should throw away in the trailer, and Jerry would drive them away the next day. Jerry turned off the lights and closed the shed.

"Let's go inside and have a cup of coffee," he said, still not asking if she cared for a cup. "Of course, tea for you." He smiled like he was proud to remember it.

"So nice of you to drop by," George exclaimed as Josie entered the living room. George and Oscar each sat in a chair facing the sofa by the large windows. It was spacious, with a stunning view over the valley. On a bright day, she was certain they could see all the way to Ashville.

"It's very nice of you to help us out with storage for the flea market," she replied.

"No problem; we don't use it."

Josie ignored the men and took a brief tour of the living room before she went over to sit down with them. The room itself looked dated, quite a few pieces of art on the wall, but no family pictures. In a corner, an old desk stood, and over it was a large old frame with lots of old keys inside it. It was a white frame, but the paint was aged into yellowish and it was crackled all around. The keys were all neatly arranged, all of them except one that was longer than the other ones around it. *So the idea of breaking up the symmetry is an old one*, Josie thought.

"It was my wife's. She could point at each one of them and they meant something to her, and in her mind, that made it decorative," George said.

"I think it's nice. It's a nice place you've got here."

"It's big for the two of us." The hope, George had told Josie once, was that Jerry should find someone and they could take over the house. Then he could move into a smaller apartment, but it hadn't happened. It could, of course, still happen, but George had abandoned any hopes of grandchildren. "I have made you some tea. It's in the kitchen. Just sit down and wait."

"No, please, just stay seated. I'll fix it myself," she said and moved over toward the kitchen door.

"Okay," he said, slightly confused. "You must remove the tea bags from the pot, and the cups are..."

"In the cupboard over the sink," Josie broke him off.

"How did you know?" George looked baffled at her.

"It's a kitchen. Nine out of ten will arrange the kitchen in the same way," she said and smiled before she entered the kitchen. The reason was pure curiosity. She had been in George's living room before. But then she hadn't thought of the fact that once there had lived a woman in this house. Something she now knew was two. She had never seen a trace of any of them. The lack of family pictures on the walls or any other sign that his wife or daughter had ever lived there puzzled her. Now she felt a need to see if the kitchen was any different. It wasn't. The kitchen was around twenty years old, so it was refurbished long after his wife died. She looked through the tea mugs, finding none that said "best mum ever" or anything like that. She at least found a flowery one far into the cupboard. It was an old one, and flower decoration was not her style, but this was her best guess of something that remained of the woman that once lived in this house.

She re-entered the living room with the flowery mug and she saw immediately George's reaction. This was a mug that stirred up emotions. Josie pretended she didn't notice. Jerry had sat down on the sofa while she was in the kitchen. She sat down on the chair at the opposite end of George's chair. They all three looked at her. Oscar had the same drooling glare as he always gave her, but the attention she got from Jerry and George was different. She was pretty sure it was the mug.

"And I have just learned that you are family," she said and looked from Oscar to George.

"Oh, yes," George replied.

"He is my uncle, but he has been more like a dad to me."

"Nah," George objected.

"I never had a father, but I had Uncle George."

Josie looked into her almost empty cup. Normally, she would finish it, and excused herself then been on her way. But she changed her mind.

"Could I have some more tea?" she asked.

## LIKE SMOKE IN THE WIND

"Sure. Do you want me to get the pot?"

"No, I can fill up my cup in the kitchen," she said, not waiting for an answer. She was halfway out of the chair when she answered the question. When she returned, both Oscar and Jerry excused themselves. Josie sat with her cup of tea and a biscuit and smiled as the two men left the living room. She guessed Oscar was a fairly regular guest, since George didn't bother to follow him to the door. Josie waited until she was certain they were gone before she spoke.

"Did I take the wrong cup?"

"No, no, no." George held both hands up in front of him and shook his head.

"But?" she continued.

"Lorna used to drink from that cup." George sighed.

"I am sorry to have troubled you," she said. She wasn't. It was quite deliberate.

"No, it's fine."

"Do you think Lorna would have wanted to be forgotten?"

"She is not forgotten," George sneered at her, waving his arms and tipping his cup while he did.

"She's not remembered either," Josie answered. "Listen to me, George," Josie said in a gentle but determined tone. "I visit a lot of people, and whenever I visit someone who has lost a child or a spouse, I can see it. On the walls, in the decorations, because the people are remembered by their loved ones. But here, there is nothing. I didn't even know you had lost a daughter. This isn't right."

"Come, I will show you something," George said at last. After getting up from his chair, he moved over to the bookcase. He pulled out an old dusty album. He came back and sat down beside Josie on the sofa and opened it up. Josie leaned slightly over to get a better view. The first pictures were in black and white. It was wedding pictures.

"Lorna was beautiful," she said.

"She was," George agreed. He flipped on through black and white wedding photos that were turning yellow on the edges and suddenly ended with a legal document.

"It's our wedding certificate."

Josie looked at the date, July in fifty-four. It was signed by the minister, and then George and Lorna, both with a nice and curly handwriting.

**19**

"You had a nice handwriting," she replied.

"Yes, I was told I wrote like a girl." George chuckled.

Josie flipped back a page to the wedding photo. "I think you should have it framed and put it up on the wall."

"I do have one framed somewhere. It was on the wall until I refurbished the living room," he said.

"Then it's time to get it back up."

George nodded.

"And Deirdre, do you have some photos of her as well?"

George closed the album and got up and put it back in the drawer. "Do you want some more tea or are you done?" he asked. His tone made it very clear that she had overstayed her welcome.

"No thanks. I think I'll better be on my way," Josie answered. George merely nodded.

# Chapter 5

Every Tuesday at eleven, the Salvation Army was filled up with women. Some of the women in Kayne had the excuse of being at work at those hours. The rest of them showed up. It was the Kayne Home League, the Army's women's meetings. A hundred years ago or so, the idea of the Home League was to give women an excuse to leave the home and give them a few hours of free time during the week. This was, of course, in a time where women were expected to stay at home, while the men could do as they pleased. In many third world countries, the Home League still was a vital tool for educating women about health, nutrition and other important topics for women. Here in the States, where women didn't need an excuse to go out or basic education, the home league in the various corps either perished or found a new relevance. In Kayne, it was the second. The Home League kept its popularity because it had found its own niche. Mind you, it was never the Salvation Army's intention that the Home League should have this newfound purpose. It sort of just happened as a result of lumping all those women together and serving them coffee. The Home League was Kayne's hub of gossip.

One would think in a place with so little going on, there wouldn't be much to gossip about. At least that had been Josie's thought, but she soon had to admit her mistake. They could gossip about everything. And since the gossip didn't need to be true, there was no actual relationship between what was going on and what rumors were passed around. This annoyed Josie a lot, and it had tempted her to shut down the whole Home League. Marge had talked some sense into her, though. "The women up here have two things, TV and gossiping, and if they don't sit here and do it, they will take their gossip elsewhere. You just make sure they at least get a word from the good book as well."

Josie had agreed and made sure she worked hard on the Bible topic for each week.

They divided the meetings into two halves. The first hour was singing, reading the scripture, and a brief talk. Then the second one was coffee and gossip. Josie would get some grumpy looks if the first half stretched for over one hour. In the beginning, Josie had miscalculated the length of the program, because she didn't realize how much longer time each song took at the Home League. Their regular piano player, Ms. Jensen, worked as a music teacher at the school in Ashville, meaning she was at work when the Home League had its meetings. So at the Home League meetings, they used the old pianist, Mrs. Bella. Bella was a highly qualified piano player. She was the one who once taught Ms. Jensen how to play, and everyone else that could play piano in Kayne, for that matter. The problem was that Bella was getting old, and nothing went fast with Bella anymore. She would need a minute or maybe two just to find the right notes, and the song itself would go at almost half of its normal speed. As a result, they couldn't have too many songs on the program.

But Josie had learned her lesson, and only fifty-five minutes had passed as Bella, from behind the piano with booming vigor, sang the last line from the chorus of 'Blessed Assurance,' slowing down on the 'all the day' and putting in a huge tremolo on 'long,' as was her custom at the end of the songs. Josie, on her side, looked desperately down at her song book on the third verse, the one they still hadn't sung and Bella obviously had forgotten about. Josie tried to get eye-contact with Bella as she made a circle in the air with her hand, to signal that they still had a verse to go. But Bella did not see Josie, leaving Josie with no choice. So when the music stopped, Josie continued: "Perfect submission..."

Finally, Bella looked up, slightly confused for a moment, before she again focused on the songbook in front of her and cheered. "I, in my Savior..."

And by that, Josie felt 'happy and blessed.' They finished the last verse and chorus, still two minutes shy of the hour mark. This resulted in all smiles around on every table as they served the coffee at exactly twelve o'clock. Josie walked down from the platform and looked for a place to sit. In the beginning, she had chosen to sit at the tables with the least gossiping just to avoid it all, or sometimes just help in the kitchen. Later on, she realized that her presence dampened the amount of rumor that was put forward, so she circulated among the worst tables. The women were always split about having Josie at their table. For one, it kind of ruined the good conversation, but on the other hand, it was almost like getting a visit by royalty. This time, she had singled out the table

## LIKE SMOKE IN THE WIND

where Peggy Moreland sat. She was one of the few working women coming regularly to the Home League. For two hours each Tuesday, she left Hoss to manage the diner. That every other woman was gossiping and she couldn't be a part of it was more than she could bear. There were no available chairs around that table; there rarely were. But Josie just found an available chair elsewhere and squeezed down in a corner, right beside Peggy.

"How nice of you to sit with us," Peggy exclaimed with a polite, fake smile. It was obvious that Josie was ruining her plans.

"What are you guys talking about?" Josie asked.

"Peggy was just talking about Jack at the flea market," Ada Olson said, and immediately received a hostile glance from Peggy.

"Oh, poor old man, he gets easily confused these days."

"Yes, exactly," Peggy said, as if it was just what she had been saying. It was clear to Josie it wasn't, but she didn't care to dig into it.

"Well, at least I learned something new. I didn't know George had a daughter."

"Oh, Deirdre, sure that's the Kayne tragedy," Ada said.

"She should have kept away from the mill. We were specifically told to stay away from there," Peggy shot in. Josie noticed the glances she got from around the tables. Talking ill of the dead wasn't sitting well even around this table.

"I don't mean to say that it's not a tragedy and all that. But she who bragged about becoming an officer in the Salvation Army." Peggy made her voice sound overly cute and waved her right hand in the air as she said "officer in the Salvation Army." Josie pondered if that was the way she was viewed as well. "Wouldn't she then be the last person one would expect to see up at the mill?"

"What's with the mill?" Josie asked.

"The youngsters used to hang out there, often drinking and smoking."

"And worse, I'll tell you," Peggy shot in.

"You used to hang there, didn't you?" Ada shot in.

"I certainly did not." Peggy shot Ada a glance that made her crumble. "I was invited up, of course. I might have even been there a time or two, but when I realized what was going on there, I never set foot there again."

"What happened to the mill?"

"Well, because of all the things that went on there, and because of the hazards of that old building, George closed it down."

"He nailed a plank over the door and told us he would change the lock to a working one."

*Kayne, March 1978*

They could hear voices from the mill, as expected on a Friday evening. He had chosen this day because then he could tell most of those hanging around there. He had asked Frank to come along. Frank had brought some planks and nails to lock it down until they could replace the lock with a working one. It was an old model, so Frank needed to order one that would fit the old door. George's initial thought had been to burn it down to the ground, but several of the locals had talked him out of it. For them, the mill was an important part of Kayne history. For the power company that now owned it, it could prove to be an expensive part as well if they needed to maintain something they could never use. Frank laid the planks and tools down outside before they stepped inside. The mill had a small room as you entered. This was on one side of the huge mill wheel. And then there were two narrow corridors on each side of the mill wheel that led to the main room. Frank and George took each hallway to ensure that no one slipped out and away from them. The squeaking on the floorboards, however, gave them away. They could hear hushing and shoveling going on inside. As they entered the main room, the kids were all lined up as in a school picture. The room was gloomy, only lit up by light streaming in through cracks and holes in the old panels.

"Hello, Uncle George," Oscar Bowers said as he casually waved at George. Jonathan looked down, hoping his father wouldn't see him. So did the rest of the kids.

"This mill is the property of the Spokane Valley Power Company, and you are now trespassing on private property." George looked at them one after the other. "And just as important, this old mill isn't safe. It could fall down anytime."

"Or burn down if you keep smoking inside here," Frank added. "Don't you think we can smell that you have been smoking inside here?"

Some of the youngsters looked even further down into the floor.

"But, Uncle, we're careful. We don't do any harm," Oscar objected.

# LIKE SMOKE IN THE WIND

"We are closing down the mill, and if I see anyone inside here, I will press charges, understood?"

Nobody answered, but they could see the occasional nodding.

"Now, get out of here and don't come back."

The youngsters got up one after the other, and one by one, they marched out.

"We'll have a talk once I'll get home," Frank said as Jonathan passed him. Oscar was the last to leave, but he said nothing as he passed his uncle.

Well outside, Frank found the planks and took them over to the door.

"Can you hold this right here?" Frank said as he placed the first plank over the door. George pushed the plank toward the door and Frank got his hammer and the nails. With four-inch nails both in the door and the door frame, he nailed the plank in place. Soon after, three planks covered the door.

"That should hold it for a while," Frank said.

"How long before you get the lock in place?"

"Two weeks, three at the most."

"And that was it?" Josie inquired.

"Not really. Rumors will have it," Peggy said. She would always phrase it like this when she tried to avoid the 'how do you know' question. "That Oscar stole a hammer, a crowbar and a metal file at his uncle's place. Then he opened it up again. He filed off most of the nails, so they looked as if they were in place, but he left only two in each plank. So when he came, he crowbarred it open and hammered it in place when he left."

"So they used the mill just as earlier?"

"No, there was never a big crowd there anymore."

"I never heard of this," Ada objected.

"Well, what I heard is that Oscar and maybe some other boys used it to lure girls up there, and you know."

Josie sat there and wondered if she had lost the calming effect she used to have on rumors, or if it was just Peggy.

"I think we'd better leave it at this and not go around accusing people of stuff we are not sure even happened."

"But I..." Peggy started.

"You said it yourself. It was a rumor that you had heard," Josie said. Peggy looked grumpily down into her coffee. *Game, set and match for me*, Josie thought.

"I'd better get back to the diner and see if Hoss needs some help," Peggy said, and got up. She wrapped an orange and blue scarf around her neck. Combined with her purple glasses and her bright red lipstick, it must have felt like a sucker punch to anyone with the slightest sense of aesthetics, but in Kayne, it was just plain Peggy. The scarf fluttered around her head as she walked down the aisle.

"I remember Peggy was very much in love with Oscar back then," Ada said, and chuckled as soon as Peggy had left. "Of course, that was before Hoss came along."

# Chapter 6

Josie had scanned through the fridge and searched inside herself for the inspiration to make a tempting dinner out of some of its contents, but found none. She could, of course, buy something else, but she feared she wouldn't find any inspiration in the grocery store either. That left her with the diner.

Kayne had in total four stores, the Salvation Army, the only church in town, and a diner. Every not so often, some out-of-towners dropped by the diner. It was most likely someone who was lost, or someone visiting relatives in town. But basically, the guests at the diner were only the locals. People in Kayne liked their diner, or that their city had a diner. So everyone would from time to time drop by and eat a meal at the diner. Josie found the diner to be a suitable alternative when she was too busy to make her own dinner. Or when she simply cared for someone to chat with during the meal. The food was good. Not the best diner on the west coast as someone bragged, but she would put it on the top ten list of places she had been. It looked like any diner she'd been to. The kitchen was in one corner of the diner, with the counter in front. Then the tables were arranged as booths by the window in an L-shape around the kitchen. She scanned the room as she entered. She came in hopes of company, the need for someone to talk to. If she didn't find anyone, she could always sit down in an empty booth and someone would join her eventually. But if she joined someone, she could choose whom to sit with. She spotted Marge at the same time Marge spotted her.

"Hello," Marge said. She waved and pointed to the seat opposite of her in her booth. Josie nodded.

"Are you here for dinner as well?"

"Yes," she said, and sat down where Marge had pointed to. "Is that the special?" Josie pointed at Marge's plate.

"It is; it's delicious."

The "today's special" was a traditional dinner, and it was also what Hoss, the chef, did best. He wasn't good at what people in Kayne labeled modern food.

Burgers and fries, for instance, was considered modern food in Kayne. Josie had tried it once and agreed with the locals that Hoss wasn't good with modern food.

"Josie, how nice to see you. What can I get you?" Peggy asked, sneaking up from behind. Peggy and Hoss ran the diner together. Hoss was the chef and Peggy was the waiter. They were quite opposites in personalities, but still a nice match for the diner. Hoss was a shy person who rarely said anything, so he mostly hid out in the kitchen. Peggy, on the other hand, loved to be the center of attention. One could, of course, debate if that was considered a good or a bad trait for a person waiting tables.

"I'll have the special," Josie said.

"One special coming up." Peggy jotted down a few letters in her notebook and returned to behind the counter.

"Good to be done with the flea market," Marge said.

"Yes. Jerry came for the remaining stuff yesterday," Josie replied. "Oscar Bowers was at George's place. I didn't know they were related."

"Oh yes, he lived with them as a teenager, or maybe even a bit older." She stopped talking and looked around before she leaned over and continued in a low whisper. "I think he had gotten into some bad company in Seattle, so his mother sent him to live with George." Marge straightened herself back up, clearly done with the secretive part of the Oscar Bowers giveaway.

It was dinnertime in Kayne, and several hungry dinner customers dropped in the door, keeping Peggy busy. As a result, Josie had to wait even longer for her dinner.

"I remember when Oscar came to town; it was exotic, with someone from the big city living in little Kayne. The boys wanted to be like him and the girls wanted to be with him." Marge looked into the air like she was picturing the old days.

"He was dashing with his long hair and fancy clothes. Something we had only seen on TV," Peggy broke in as she served Josie's dinner.

"I guess he was around seventeen the first time he came to stay with George. In the beginning, it was just a few weeks at the time. Then his stays were longer and longer. But he really didn't move until you know who passed away." Marge made her mouth small and tilted her head along with the last statement, to emphasize compassion. Josie wondered if she needed to explain Harry Potter

# LIKE SMOKE IN THE WIND

to her soldiers, because "you know who" was not a good analogy. Josie left the topic altogether and focused on her meal. She realized that she should have asked what the special was before ordering it, because she had no idea what she was about to eat. But it smelled good, and it had mashed potatoes. Hoss made a good mash.

"Do you know what we're eating?" she asked upon tasting the first bite.

"Don't you like it?"

"Oh yes, I like it a lot. That's why I would like to know what it is."

"It's a beef stew. Irish, I think it is. He used to put beer in it, but I talked him out of it." She straightened her back in pure pride.

"So I'm good?"

"You're good, my dear," Marge replied and didn't take notice of the slight irony in Josie's voice.

"And Oscar and the other boys..." Peggy had apparently served the other dinner guests and came to take part in the conversation they already had finished. "Do you know what they did?"

Josie shook her head.

"It's pretty silly, but you know what boys are like, don't you? They made a top five list of the prettiest girls in our school. Can you believe it?"

Josie shook her head again, focusing more on eating her dinner than hearing Peggy's gossip of the past.

"It was Deirdre, of course. Everyone liked her," she continued without thinking the listeners might not be interested. Josie had not yet seen any photos of Deirdre, but if she was as pretty as her mother, she could easily see how Deirdre would fit on a top five list.

"Then it was Mary Ohlson, and two girls from Ashville." She paused as an opera singer would right before the grand finale. "And me. It was so embarrassing."

"Tell Hoss he makes an excellent beef stew. Is it Irish?" Josie said in an attempt to derail the entire conversation.

"The boys made a challenge about who could date most of the top five girls. But apart from the Ashville girls, they didn't succeed very well. Of course, Hoss managed to date me," she said and giggled. It amazed Josie how a story that started with how Oscar moved to Kayne could end up with how Hoss and Peggy hooked up. At least Peggy was done talking and moved on to other customers.

"The boys?" Josie asked and looked at Marge.

"Oscar, Hoss, Frank Meadows, Jack and even Ernie. Those were the boys at the approximate same age."

"What about Jerry?"

"No, Jerry was much younger. I seem to remember he and Carl used to hang out a lot. But I think they were the only two boys at the same age from Kayne. So it was normal that they would hang out."

Josie thought about Jerry and Carl. Today, it seemed like they were worlds apart. Jerry living with his father in that grand house and Carl in his little cabin up by the dam.

"I think, however, they stopped hanging out that much after you know what. Carl dropped out of school not long after. I guess that must have been the reason," she said and scratched her chin as if it helped her memory. Josie said nothing.

"It broke Jack's heart, it really did. Their grandmother's too, for that matter."

"Oh, that reminds me. I mustn't forget to drop by Jack. I've been meaning to talk to him," Josie said.

"Jack? You won't get a sensible word out of him," Peggy broke in. She wasn't further away than she could eavesdrop on every conversation at once.

"Sure you can. I just need to find him in a clear moment. I need to talk to him about what he said at the flea market."

"Good luck with that," Peggy said, but she was already on her way, so Josie wasn't sure if the comment was meant for her, or for someone else.

# Chapter 7

Josie considered herself a city girl, and way out of her element in a rural small town such as Kayne. Still, living in Kayne had its perks. One of them was jogging. Just about a quarter of a mile from her apartment, she was on various forest trails. Another one, she had learned, was that most of the trails were up hills. She could run as far as she could upwards and then only have down hills going home. She had the routine of running several nights in the week before bedtime. Much of her work was about interacting with people, and in a lot of these interactions, they served cakes. And most times, people would be offended if she didn't eat any. Running was her way to even out all the cakes. If not, she feared she would grow out of all her clothing. In addition, the late-night run cleared her head.

The trails were made of packed gravel that cut through the forest. Her favorite ran in a circle around Kayne on the west side, going down the Silver Lake Road on her way back. This trail wasn't as steep, and it had quite a few openings in the wall of leaves that surrounded the trail. It was just her, focusing on her breathing and the rhythmical sound of feet hitting down on the gravel. Every time she passed one opening, she turned and admired the view, and the wind greeted her face as she did.

Moving into the forest again, she could still hear the wind shaking the branches above her, as the only sound that accompanied the repeated sound of trainers touching down on gravel. At the top of the trail where the trail turned and headed in toward the road, she was a few hundred yards over the highest positioned houses in Kayne. Her breathing got lighter as the road leveled out. The first times she ran here, she had walked the last bit to the top. Now, a year later, it satisfied her to register that her stride didn't slow down during the long uphill.

The forest, as well as the trail, ended with the road. On the other side of the road, the river that had been so important for Kayne. She stopped, looking into the river. It narrowed in just below the trail, and an old ruin stood there.

She had seen it countless times before, but now that she knew what it was, it made her heart skip a beat. It was the old mill, an over forty-year-old fire site. The stone structures on it were fairly intact, but barely any of the wooden structures. Left from the mill wheel was just a solid rusty metal beam placed in the stone shafts, where the stone walls forced the river together. It had probably started its decay well before the fire. She crossed the road and balanced onto the stone wall. Not knowing how safe it was, she treaded lightly. Some wooden beams that once had supported the floor were still in place, but she was far from tempted to try them out. Every single one of them was overgrown with moss and grass and revealed little evidence of a fire.

"You're inspecting the mill, I see." A strange, dark voice from behind her almost made her trip. She turned and saw a dark figure appear on the road.

"Who's there?" she answered.

"It is I, George," the voice said, and as he got off the road and approached her, she could recognize his face, but his voice still sounded odd in the wind.

"You scared me," she said and smiled with relief as she walked toward him.

"What are you doing here?" George asked.

"I don't know." She stopped so she could look at George when she spoke. She didn't dare balance on the old uneven stone structure without checking where she placed her foot. "I've passed this place so many times and never known what it is. Now I know what it is, and what it means." She looked down and almost mumbled the last words.

"Now you know," George repeated. Josie walked the last two steps on the stone wall and jumped off and onto the grass. Then she walked up toward George but stopped a few yards away from him, and turned back toward the ruin. They both stood there and looked at the remains of the old mill.

"Let me remind you that this is still private property, and no place to be playing." George sounded hostile. Josie figured he still was angry at her for pushing him on Deirdre the day before.

"I wasn't playing," Josie answered bluntly. It annoyed her when the old people here treated her like a girl. George was far from the only one doing that.

"No, you're not playing. You just pry into other people's misfortune." Josie could feel the hostility in his words. "Why can't you just leave us alone?" he continued.

# LIKE SMOKE IN THE WIND

This was probably a good idea, but whenever Josie was treated condescendingly, and accused of something she was not, an urge to defend herself always kicked in. She turned toward George and pointed straight at him.

"Sure, let's pretend it all never happened. How's that been working out for you?"

"Well, that is my business, and mine alone. It's my life and I choose what's best for me." George was red in his face, and for a split second, Josie wondered if he was about to attack her physically.

"It is not just your business. Can't you see how it is affecting everyone around you?"

"You know nothing about this," he lashed out at her.

"Well then, educate me!" Josie looked at him with the determination of someone in a staring contest. George snorted before he walked away. He was almost back on the road when he stopped. Josie could see the contours of him in the setting sun, that his shoulders were rising and falling with his breathing.

"I closed the mill because I feared a tragic accident. That the old structure would collapse over someone. I even thought it might burn down, after all the youngsters were smoking when they were at the mill," George said, still with his back to Josie.

"I really could picture that scenario, but never had I dreamt it would be Deirdre." George turned toward Josie. His usually collected appearance had crumbled and become somewhat softer. "She was never amongst the kids up in the mill, and she sure didn't smoke." George tilted his head and looked out into the air. It was a habit of his whenever he was reminiscing. "She hated smoking. She once caught Jerry smoking."

*Kayne 1978*

Deirdre had done her chores of the day, her homework, and made dinner. Jerry had disappeared right after dinner without considering his own homework. She had hurried because she had agreed to come over to Lissie after dinner, guessing she'd better deal with Jerry not doing his homework later. She stopped in the crossing between Silver Lake Road and Hunter Street, where

Lissie lived. On the other side of the road, down a grassy slope to the river, there were two giant boulders. She listened as the wind blew her long blond curly hair in every direction. The wind was always blowing up here. She thought she'd heard something. Then she heard it once more. It was boys laughing, coming from the river, from behind the boulders. She kept listening and now she could hear the boy's laughter even clearer. The voices were familiar. It was Jerry and Carl. She snuck down the slope. She would teach Jerry a lesson for sneaking out before doing his homework.

The boulders were placed so they formed a triangle with the river and was a great hideout. Deirdre got around on the other side of the boulders to find out they weren't only skipping homework, they were smoking. The two boys reacted in opposite ways upon seeing Deirdre. Carl threw away his cigarette and ran other direction, soaking his shoes, as his escape forced him into the river. Jerry froze. He just sat there and stared at the glowing cigarette. Deirdre walked toward him and stepped on Carl's still glowing cigarette on the grass. She heard Carl running up the slope back on to the road. She'd deal with him later. A talk with Grandma Sutton would settle that matter. Now she would deal with Jerry, she thought, and looked him straight in his eyes. Jerry did not look back; he just kept his focus on the glow.

"I don't know where to begin. I'm just so disappointed in you. First, you run off without doing your homework." She moved slowly toward him. "Then you go out here and smoke cigarettes with Carl?" She pulled the cigarette out of his hand, and their eyes met in a brief moment before he looked down to the ground. She dropped the cigarette to the ground and stepped on it. Then she slapped Jerry in the face. He looked up, and she saw the glittering of a tear in the corner of his eyes. She didn't know if it was because of the slap or if it was remorse. "You're twelve, for heaven's sake. Where did you get cigarettes from?"

"From Oscar; he asked if I wanted to try it one day. And after that, he'd kept asking if I care for a cig."

"She was furious, more so than I was. I guess it was because she was a soldier. You have a much more strict policy on smoking than the rest of us."

# LIKE SMOKE IN THE WIND

Josie nodded. The Salvation Army had a strict policy on smoking. It was one thing she liked about the Army.

"She made me ground Jerry for an entire week. Jerry was a pain in the neck all week." George chuckled. "A week and a half later, I remember it must have been, because Jerry was grounded from Wednesday to Wednesday, and this was on a Sunday. She came to talk to me about Oscar. He was living with us a bit on and off those days. She wanted me to send him back to Seattle because he was giving cigarettes to Jerry. That was clearly an overreaction," George said, and lifted his hands up in the air.

"Giving cigarettes to kids is bad, but maybe not that bad."

"I promised her I'd have a talk with him." George looked blankly out into the air and slowly shook his head. "It is always tragic when young people die, but Deirdre..." His voice cracked briefly before he swallowed and breathed and slowly regained control and turned back to his usual demeanor.

"You know, losing first your wife and then your daughter in a few years, that can really break a man."

"I can only imagine," Josie said in a nearly inaudible voice, and wasn't sure if he'd heard it.

"But I still had Jerry to care for. I couldn't break down. I had to carry on." He turned back toward the road once more. "I put a lid on everything and buried the pain. Maybe that is not the best way to deal with it, but it was the only way I knew." He stopped talking as if he waited for a response that never came. "This is my way, and I need you to respect that." Now George didn't wait for a response, but walked away and disappeared down Silver Lake Road.

# Chapter 8

At first, the distant wailing just blended into her dreams, but as the sirens grew closer, they woke her up. She sat up in her bed, still dizzy after sleeping, trying to sort out what was a dream and what was reality. The sirens grew closer. They were definitely real. Josie got out of bed and peeked out of the window just in time to see two fire trucks passing below her window. She rubbed her tired eyes and gazed down the street after the trucks. The flames rose high in the air, but she couldn't make out what house it was. It didn't matter. Any house burning would be the house of a friend in this tiny town. She got dressed in a hurry, and was on her way out the door as an idea struck her. Josie turned around and went into the kitchen, and started making coffee. Fifteen minutes later, she was on her way with two large thermoses with coffee. She went out into the night. The smell of burnt wood and the crackles from flames filled the air as she hastened down the stairs from the main entrance.

She was not the first coming to the site. There was already a large crowd circling around the two fire trucks. It was Jack's house, and it was in full flames. She had feared this. They all had. Jack Sutton was really not the man to live on his own, but nothing could ever take him away from that house. Everyone in Kayne feared that with his level of dementia and living on his own, it was only a matter of time before some kind of accident would happen. Friends of his had even made a schedule where they took turns checking up on him. Still, the accident happened, and it was probably the worst kind of accident. Josie plowed her way through the crowd and addressed the nearest firefighter.

"Excuse me, sir, but can you tell me who's in charge here?" she asked.

"It's Chief Henderson," he replied and pointed toward two men talking together. One of them looked like he was the one giving orders to the other, so Josie guessed this had to be Henderson.

"Chief Henderson," Josie said. "I am Lieutenant Josie Facundo in the Salvation Army of Kayne."

"Nice to meet you," Henderson replied.

## LIKE SMOKE IN THE WIND

"I brought some coffee, and if there is something we can assist with, just say the word."

"Bless you," he said. "We have to assess the situation, and I will tell you if we need anything. Coffee, however, is always welcomed." The chief smiled.

Josie poured him a cup, which he greeted with a smile.

"Are they going in to look for Jack?" Josie asked and pointed at two firefighters putting on their SCBA.

"Not yet. It's still too dangerous to send someone upstairs before we know if the floor is bearing. The stairs to the basement is also a risk."

"And the first floor?"

"We could probably send someone in on the first floor pretty soon. But that doesn't help much if he is on the second floor," Chief Henderson said, and shrugged.

"But I don't think Jack was anywhere else but on the first floor." Josie turned around and searched with her eyes after someone who could confirm it for her. "Ernie," she shouted and waved him over to her and the fire chief. Ernie was one of those old friends that used to check up on him.

"Ernie, was Jack ever in the basement or on the second floor?"

"No, not for several years," he answered. "You see, we have feared an accident for a long time, so we have locked the door to the basement and closed off the stairs to the second floor with several ropes in the stairway. We did that after he fell down the stairs two, almost three years ago."

"Then I guess it's worth checking out the first floor," Henderson said. He went over to the hose crews and gave some instructions before he went over to the firefighters getting ready to enter the building. Meanwhile, one hose was pumping water directly into the first floor.

It felt like forever before the firefighters came out. The firefighters had pushed the crowd further away from the fire. Everyone except Josie, who now stood right behind the firefighters with her thermos of coffee, and waited for the firefighters to come out. The heat from the fire was burning in her face, and she couldn't imagine how it would be for the men actually inside the building. Finally, they came out without Jack. They shook their heads as if to say they had found no one.

Chief Henderson turned toward Josie. "He wasn't on the first floor. So unless we find him somewhere else, we assume he is still in the building."

Josie nodded.

"Is there anywhere else he can be?"

"We can arrange a search-party for him," Josie said.

"Good, do that, but if you don't find him, we will have to search the rest of the building as soon as it is safe."

Josie stepped over to the crowd, watching the fire.

"Can I please have your attention?" she shouted.

"Be quiet," Jonathan Meadows shouted even louder. "The lieutenant has something to say."

After a few "hushes" around the crowd, it finally went quiet. Josie explained the situation and called for volunteers to the search-party. Everyone with legs that were fresh enough volunteered.

"You need to find some flashlights, and some of you need better shoes. Then you guys all need to come back here to be assigned an area to search."

The crowd scattered in to each their direction, and only a few people remained.

"Ernie, get me a town map and a pen."

"Sure thing," Ernie said and was on his way. When he came back with the map, the two first volunteers already waited to be assigned a search area. They were among the older volunteers, so Josie sent them to search on the nearby roads. Then Jonathan Meadows came.

"I brought some extra flashlights from the store," he said and showed her a plastic bag full of flashlights.

"Good, that will come in handy," she replied. "You and Hoss can search through the southern trails." She pointed at Hoss, who came right behind Jonathan. As the volunteers came in, Josie assigned them an area and checked it out on the map. As all became quiet, Carl Sutton approached slowly. "Anything I can do?"

Thoughts rushed through Josie's mind. Carl was Jack's cousin, but they were both raised in that very house as brothers by their grandmother. Everyone knew what Jack meant to Carl, and how this had to be for him. Josie reckoned it probably was better to do something than nothing.

"Sure, you can help with the search."

"But I don't have a flashlight. It's too far up to my cabin."

# LIKE SMOKE IN THE WIND

"No problem, I've got one for you," she said and reached for one in Jonathan's bag.

"Can I help with something?" It was Jerry Chisholm. His hair was up in all directions, and he yawned as he spoke. "My father woke me up and told me to come over."

"Good. Do you have a flashlight?"

"Yup," he said and turned it on and off.

"You and Carl here can take the southern trails." She had already sent Jonathan and Hoss that way, but all the places were full, and that was a large area, so she reckoned a few more pairs of eyes wouldn't hurt.

As the entire search-party was sent out, she sent Ann and Marge to the Salvation Army to prepare a breakfast for the volunteers as they came back.

The day was dawning as the first ones returned. She crossed them off on the map and sent them to the Army Hall for some breakfast. None came back with news of Jack.

"We are ready to make a full-house search," Chief Henderson informed Josie, "but give us a notice if he is found, then we can call it off."

"I will," she replied. The flames were far from as visible now as they used to be, but it was still burning hot. "Good luck."

"Thanks," the chief replied, already on his way toward the burning building.

# Chapter 9

The smell of smoke diminished as the corps hall grew closer. It had to be just before dawn, and the sky above the mountains in the east brightened. She could hear voices inside. Not too jolly, neither too sad. It sounded like a good but dampened mood. It had all the requisites of a good time. They had all done a job together for a good cause and now they enjoyed a meal together. But the uncertainty of Jack's faith lay thick in the air. Josie pushed the door open and the smell of coffee and fried bacon greeted her. Margie and Ann had put several tables together on one long table in the second hall. About half of the search party was still there. A quick look and Josie saw that most of the ones still lingering were those who had to go to work in an hour or so. Josie reckoned they had stayed and took a long breakfast at the Army. After all, they wouldn't get any sleep anyway. Marge caught her eyes and her face asked for news, but Josie didn't respond. She scanned the faces around the table, but Carl wasn't among them. She settled for Jerry. She knelt down beside him and patted him on his shoulder. He turned and his eyes didn't look as tired as they had done earlier.

"Where's Carl?" she asked.

"He was tired. I drove him home."

"Okay. How did he take it?"

"He was pretty desperate. He was checking and double checking everywhere. I tried to tell him it was pointless, but he just wouldn't listen."

"Well, you can't really blame him, can you?"

"No, I guess not."

Josie got up, and now everyone was aware of her presence. The chatting had silenced, and they all looked at her, everyone with the same question painted on their faces. Josie said nothing. She just walked slowly to the end of the table. She stood for a while, nervously fidgeting with her fingers, with all eyes on her.

"You already know that the search came up with nothing." Josie swallowed before she could go on. "I just spoke with Chief Henderson."

## LIKE SMOKE IN THE WIND

Everyone waited for an answer; most of them had already guessed. The silence was pressing and Josie struggled to find voice enough to utter the words. "They found a dead body in the basement." Her words were hoarse and almost as a whisper. "It's male, and it's assumed to be Jack." She sat down and looked at the crowd. Henderson had told her that the body was in front of the basement stairs, lying face down. He had most likely fallen down the stairs, but Josie didn't feel like conveying that.

Josie sat in silence and looked at the others as if they were in a bubble and Josie was outside looking in on them. This entire night had prepared them for the news, but they still couldn't believe it. Of course, this was Kayne. In this small town, people died of natural causes. Probably not even in Kayne, but at the local hospital or retirements home in Ashville, the neighboring city. Had this happened only a week ago, it would be the first unnatural death she had heard of in Kayne. But of course, now she had also heard of Deirdre. She also died in a fire. Josie's mind wondered about the odds of everyone dying of unnatural causes died in fires. Probably not that high, she figured. It drew her back to the people in the bubble. The voices were raised. They talked about the key to the basement, who had forgotten to lock the door, or not hidden the key after locking. Soon after, accusations were thrown back and forth over the table.

"Stop!" Josie stood up and shouted with her full lungs. "This is not a time or place for this kind of talk. As far as we're concerned, this was a tragic accident and nothing more. We all knew that this could happen, and finding someone to blame doesn't bring him back." Josie was all red in her face and the silence was back in the hall.

"She is right, we can't let this town be torn to pieces every time an accident occurs," Ernie broke the silence.

"I really got my hopes up when they didn't find him on the first floor," Hoss said. Several of the others nodded and added some humming noises. Josie knew how they felt. She had rejoiced inside when they didn't find him on the first floor. Somehow she had expected them to find him cold and delirious, lying in a ditch. Then they would get him some warm clothes and coffee and everything would turn out just fine, but that didn't happen.

"I'm Inspector Fred Becker from the Spokane Sheriff Department. I heard Chief Henderson was available here." Fred Becker was a tall man. He wore a cheap suit, cowboy boots, and a large white cowboy hat. If there were any cliches on a country lawman, this was it. A uniformed police officer stood right behind him. He looked chubby against Fred's tall and lean stature, without really being chubby. Only a few firefighters were left at the site to guard against any new outburst; the rest enjoyed a well-earned breakfast at the Salvation Army.

"At your service, Inspector," Henderson replied without getting out of his chair. "You're here to investigate the fire, I presume."

"Standard procedure," Fred said. He took off his hat and moved toward the table with the firefighters.

"Do you care for some coffee?" Marge broke in.

"That would be nice," the inspector answered and found a chair right opposite of Chief Henderson. He swirled it around and straddled over it, leaning his chest into the backrest. "Is there anything you can tell me at this point?"

"Not much. We must make sure the fire is fully out before we can do any investigations on the nature of the fire. Probably not before tomorrow."

Fred nodded and took a sip of the coffee Marge had brought him.

"There's a dead body, presumably the resident, but we can't say for certain. We can't even tell if he died in the fire or before."

"How come?" Fred Becker leaned forward, resting both elbows on the table, and scratched his chin.

"He lay at the end of the stairs. He may have fallen down before the fire, or at least before the fire became lethal."

"I see." Fred nodded but kept his hand on his chin. "We will talk to the neighbors and relatives while it's fresh in their minds. But we won't do much more than that before we have a cause of fire and the autopsy report."

"Can take some days. It's not a priority autopsy."

"And how long will you take?" Fred got up from his chair and finished his cup standing.

"We just want to wrap things up here; a few days, tops."

"Good," Fred replied. The other police officer got up as well. "Thanks for the coffee," Fred said and placed the coffee cup on the table. "The resident..."

## LIKE SMOKE IN THE WIND

"Jack Sutton." Josie had been in the kitchen helping Marge out with the dishes after the long breakfast for the entire search party, and now the firefighters. Now she appeared in the kitchen door to see if the firefighters were about to finish the breakfast.

"What?" Fred looked slightly confused at Josie.

"The resident, his name is Jack Sutton."

Fred nodded. "And you might be?"

"Lieutenant Facundo. I'm in charge of the Salvation Army's work here in Kayne." She moved toward the inspector with an outstretched hand. Fred greeted her, saying nothing.

"And his cousin?"

"Carl Sutton." Josie stepped back a few steps to avoid standing awkwardly close to the inspector.

"Do you, by any chance, have his address?"

"Is Kayne good enough?"

"Maybe some kind of direction?"

"Sure, you drive all the way up to the dam, and then you'll know you have gone too far, so you need to turn and go back down. Then it's the first to the right," Josie said and smiled. "Of course, it's not really a road. It's more like an opening in the bushes that makes room for a car, more or less."

"Okaaay..." Fred Becker looked uncomfortable following Josie's road description.

"I'm going up to Carl after I'm done with the dishes. I could give you a lift."

The inspector mumbled something to himself, considering Josie's offer. "Will it take long before you are ready?"

"You can just go. I've got this," Marge shot in.

# Chapter 10

Fred sent the other police officer off to talk with the neighbors while Josie and Fred drove up to Carl's cabin. Fred, of course, insisted that they ride in his car, a big black Ford that raised suspicions driving through the quiet streets. And seeing Josie riding with the inspector from Spokane would surely end up as the daily gossip. Every prospect of a romantic partner to Josie, no matter how farfetched, fueled every gossiper in town.

"I heard you're from LA," Fred said.

"Sure," Josie answered. Of course, he had heard that she was a big-town girl all the way from LA. It was probably the single most exotic thing that ever happened in Kayne.

"How is it living in a tiny city?"

In order to kick-start a conversation, one always starts off with some basic question. Josie had heard the reason for this was to find some common ground to converse about. Her problem was that it always revolved around the big-city-girl-in-tiny-city theme, and she was getting tired of it.

"You tell me, Mr. Spokaner."

"Fair point," Fred responded. "I guess Spokane is a small town compared to LA."

"No, I'm just kidding. Spokane is good. I go there when I miss the city essentials."

"Such as?"

"Pretty basic stuff, really. A movie theater, junk food and there's a lot of food I can't get around here. The local grocery store's idea of exotic spices is basil."

"I can see the need for some junk food now and then, but I tend to agree with the grocery store on the spices," Fred said, and chuckled. "I never go beyond salt and pepper."

"You sound like a bachelor."

"Sure am, ma'am. Guess I'm not ready to be tied down right yet."

## LIKE SMOKE IN THE WIND

"I hate to bring this up, but you do live in Spokane."

Josie laughed. Fred nodded to say he got her point, but he didn't laugh.

"You've got to slow down a bit or we are going to overshoot the road."

Fred slowed down, but not fast enough.

"Stop, stop," Josie said. Fred brought the car to a full stop and gave her a confused expression.

"Really? That's the exit?" He backed up about thirty yards and then he squeezed the car through the shrubbery onto what might have been a road a long time ago. Carl's cabin was an old hunter's lodge up on the mountain. He hadn't done more than absolutely necessary repairs on it since he got it quite a few years ago, and it looked like it was the paint that was holding it together.

"That's it?"

"That's it," Josie replied as Fred pulled up beside Carl's beat up little pickup. "There's one thing I need to tell you before we enter. Carl is Kayne's troubled soul, and today, he is most likely more troubled than ever."

He was.

What started out as a gentle knocking on the door grew into light slamming with no response. Finally, they heard something rambling about inside. Josie went in, Fred stayed put. She looked at him as she entered through the door. He said nothing, just gave her a face that said it all. Police can't really go barging in on strangers. Not without a search warrant, but this was not that kind of house call. The other reason to barge in was if he feared for someone's life, and the sounds from inside suggested nothing even close. Josie shrugged and walked in as if she owned the place. Technically, a Salvation Army officer couldn't just walk into people's houses either, but Josie was getting used to this. If she didn't see or hear from Carl for a couple of days, she would go up to his cabin and make him some food.

"You're early. I just hit the bottle last night." Carl was lying in an old beat-up recliner in the corner of the tiny living room.

"I am, but I need you back on your feet quite soon." She walked toward him, passing tables with all sorts of stuff placed upon them. Carl was a handyman, living on doing simple repairs for people, or he would get stuff that was broken, fixed it and sold it. People said he had a knack for it. The only broken thing he couldn't fix was himself. The living room also served as his workshop, which explained all the stuff. On and around the large table in the center of the living room, there were old radios, tables lacking a foot or dressers missing the drawer knobs, and a large variety of kitchen appliances, much of which Josie recognized from the flea market. The entire living room was like a maze of stuff. If the flea market had been a mess, it was nothing like Carl's living room. The flea market was as important for Carl's livelihood as it was for the Salvation Army in Kayne. In addition to always getting good prices on the stuff he bought, they would give him all kinds of electrical items that didn't work. It had amazed Josie how many people would donate things to the flea market that didn't work. She wondered if it could be labeled a donation if they basically got rid of trash. But in the hands of Carl, it came back to life and he could sell it.

"I'm going to make you some coffee. What do you think about that?"

Carl nodded in approval, and Josie made her way to the kitchen and got the kettle going.

"By the way, there's a sheriff coming in from the city. He would like to see you," she shouted into the living room. Carl just grunted an answer.

"Can I let him in?"

"Sure, whatever," Carl said.

Josie came back from the kitchen and smiled as she passed Carl on her way to the door.

"You can come inside now, Inspector," she said as she opened the door for Fred Becker.

"Thanks," he said and stepped by her into the living room. He furrowed his brows as he looked at all the stuff.

"Sit down," Carl mumbled as he tried to maneuver himself into a seated position. Fred pulled out a stool from underneath the table and sat down.

"Are you Carl Sutton?" he asked.

"Yeah." Carl grunted more than he spoke, along with a single nod.

"Did you hear about the fire down in Kayne last night?"

Carl looked at the inspector long and hard before he answered. "What you think I'm doing? Drinking because my favorite lost out in *America's Got Talent*?"

"So you are aware that Jack Sutton's house burnt to the ground," Fred continued in the same composed manner.

Carl nodded.

"Would you care for some coffee, Inspector?" Josie asked from the kitchen.

# LIKE SMOKE IN THE WIND

"No thanks, I'm good," Fred replied.

"Good call; I'm terrible at making coffee."

"She really is. I don't drink it unless I'm loaded." Carl laughed at his own joke.

"I am sorry to inform you that there was a dead body found in the fire ruins. We haven't done any identification yet, but most likely, it is your cousin." Fred was keeping a formal tone.

"So, do you need me to identify him or something?"

Fred said nothing. The silence was eventually broken off when Josie came in with the coffee. She placed the cup in Carl's hands and supported him on the first sip. "Be careful, it's hot," she warned.

Carl took a tiny sip and then another slightly larger one. He held the cup with two trembling hands, and Josie supported his hands with hers. She looked up into his foggy expression.

"Mr. Sutton," Fred said, almost in a whisper. "I am afraid the body is severely burned." Josie could see how the police inspector struggled with his words.

Carl nodded slightly, and Josie helped him to another sip.

The coffee might not be tasty, but it did the job, and Carl regained some more focus.

"Can you tell me when you last saw Jack Sutton?" Fred asked.

"Why? Do you expect any foul play?"

"No, but we do a routine investigation whenever someone dies in a fire."

"I had dinner with him two days ago."

"How was he then?"

"His usual. He was kind of living in the past, talking on and on about our youth. You know," Carl said and made a gesture with his hand that almost made him lose the cup in his lap. Josie was on the cup and took it away from him and placed it on a little coffee table beside his chair.

"He's got that disease, you know. Where you forget everything." He stared blankly into the air and tears showed up in the corner of his eyes. "He had..."

"I've heard," Fred said and nodded. "You did not see him yesterday?"

"No, not on Tuesdays." Carl sighed, wiped his eyes, and reached for his cup. He leaned toward the little coffee table and, with trembling hands, he took a sip of coffee. Josie helped him place the cup back on the table.

47

## ISAAC LIND

"You see, we had this system. Sometimes I ate with him and other times he ate with someone else."

"Do you know who?"

"No, I'm not sure. They're a group that takes turns inviting him."

"So you're the only one that ate dinner with him at his place."

"Well, he couldn't remember the glasses on his own nose. He couldn't cook anything. So I guess it was easier for the others to make dinner in their own home and invite him over." Carl reached for the coffee cup and tentatively moved his head forward, trying to reach the cup until Josie took the hint and helped him to another sip. "But I grew up in that very house, so for me, it always felt like home. So I liked to come down there and cook for him."

Josie glanced around the messy living room and could easily come up with one more reason he preferred to eat down at Jack's place instead of having Jack up in the cabin.

"So you're the only one that actually was in his house?"

"No, no, there was always someone checking in on him."

"Do you know who?"

"No, could be anyone. His key was in his door on the outside. Anyone could lock themselves in."

"Always?"

"Yup."

Fred looked bewildered up at Josie, then just smiled and nodded back to him..

"They do have a list of some kind, but it doesn't include me," Carl said and nodded toward the bottle on the tiny table. It was easy to see how Carl's inclination toward alcohol would make him too unreliable to look after a demented old man. But there was also a hint of pain in the statement, the pain of not being there for the only relative he had.

"You hang in there," Fred said, and tapped him on his shoulder as he got up from the stool.

"Should have been me, you know."

Fred was already halfway out the door when he turned back. "What did you say?"

"I am a bad person. I should have died in the fire. Then Jack could have a good life."

# LIKE SMOKE IN THE WIND

"I guess that's not up to us to decide, Carl," Fred said. "Now you take care."

# Chapter 11

Ernie always got a little nervous if Josie came to visit while Ann was working at the store. He felt a certain obligation to serve something to his visitors, but really wasn't capable of putting something together. Josie knew this and had insisted she only needed tea. Boiling water Ernie could manage, but Josie had to do the tea bag trick herself. He invited her into the kitchen and gave her the choice of three different tea bags. Not a hard choice. One was an herbal infusion, meaning it was not actual tea. The other contained mint, and Josie wasn't fond of mint-tasting tea. The third was an ordinary black tea, not her favorite brand, but if she let it brew a bit shorter, it would work.

"So terrible this thing with Jack," Ernie said. "How long we've feared something like this would happen."

It had been a talking point since she arrived to Kayne that Jack should not live alone. They had made several attempts to persuade Jack to move to the retirement home in Ashville, but Jack wouldn't hear of it.

"It is," Josie said as she dipped the tea bag up and down in the water before she removed the bag. It had been less than two years ago that she had been in training college, being taught about conducting funerals and caring for the grieving. One of the biggest problems with funerals, she recalled, was that the person to be buried was most likely a person she wouldn't know. How it could be easy to trivialize someone's passing if the person was old and sick, and forgetting that for someone this was the dearest person they knew. This was not at all the issue. She felt she knew Jack well, and she really cared for him. Jack had no family in town apart from Carl, who had more than enough with his own issues. So Jack had turned to the Army in those situations in which others would turn to their families. So even if he never remembered her real name, he remembered the officer was someone he could turn to.

"Is everything all right?" Ernie asked and laid a hand on her shoulder as she stood frozen by the kitchen counter, holding the tea bag in midair.

# LIKE SMOKE IN THE WIND

"This will be my first funeral, and I don't really have a clue what to do," she said. She put the tea bag into the trash and hoped he wouldn't dig any deeper.

"You'll be fine. There's an undertaker in Ashville that we should contact. This is normally the family's job, but in this case, Carl will need some help."

Josie nodded, still having the picture of a dead drunk Carl fresh in her memory. She took a teacup and found a place by the kitchen table. Ernie already had a cup and thermos of coffee there that Josie suspected was made by Ann before she left in the morning.

"I can contact the undertaker, and arrange with Carl for all the papers that need to be signed," Ernie said.

"Thank you. That will be great." Josie pulled a legal pad out of her bag and started taking notes.

"You need to talk to Marge about the practicalities around the reception."

"Reception?" Josie looked at Ernie. She had thought of the funeral, not that she would have to tackle the reception after as well.

"It's a Kayne tradition that everyone helps out with a reception, but it's always been the officers that have organized it."

Josie raised her eyebrows. The corps officer job-description was continually added to.

"Talk to Marge about that. She knows all about it," Ernie said and smiled.

He was one of those positive people that never saw a problem in anything. Sometimes this was highly encouraging, and other times, it was most annoying. Josie wrote: 'reception - talk to Marge.'

"Then we must ask Ms. Jensen to play piano. She has to take an unpaid leave from her school, so we usually pay her to compensate for her loss."

"Sure," Josie said and made a note.

"Then, it's the funeral. The sermon is in safe hands. You are a solid preacher, Lieutenant."

"Thanks," she said and blushed slightly at the compliment she wasn't sure she agreed on.

"Then you need to talk to Carl about songs. Maybe you should talk to people close to him as well. I don't know if Carl knows very much about suitable songs. And the eulogy, you should confer with Carl, but maybe you also need to talk with some of his friends about that as well."

"Like who?"

51

"Jonathan is almost the same age as Jack, and they worked together all these years. Apart from him, you can ask practically anyone. Everyone knew Jack."

"So then I'll start by asking you. Can you tell me something about Jack?"

Ernie smiled. "I don't know if I'm the best, but of course there's always something." He got up and stood a few seconds to regain his balance before he slowly moved over the living room floor over to the double bookshelf by the far wall. He looked at the books a little while before he pulled out an album. "I have some pictures of him from his youth," he said. He stopped in the doorway to the kitchen before he talked, and didn't continue toward her before he had finished talking.

"Of course it's not like today when you take pictures of everything, but we got some." Ernie pulled his chair over to Josie's side so they could look in the album together. He opened it and Josie could easily time the pictures to the seventies. They had wide pants and colorful shirts. But the boys still had short hair except one.

"Who's that?" Josie pointed at the long-haired guy.

"That's Oscar. We're a bit conservative up here, and we boys thought of long hair as quite girly. But him coming from the big city had this long hair that we'd only seen on TV."

Ernie shook his head, like he still couldn't wrap his head around the boys with long hair thing.

"That's Jack," he said and pointed to a young boy. "This was from a youth meeting at the Army."

"And where are you?"

"Behind the camera, I suppose. I don't have many pictures with me in them."

"Is Ann there?"

"No, she is five years younger than me. She was just a little girl then. That is a few years before she caught my interest."

Ernie flipped to the next page.

"And there's Jack," he said and pointed at one picture where he was standing and posing, almost leaning into a girl.

"Who's the girl?"

"Oh, that's Deirdre, poor child."

## LIKE SMOKE IN THE WIND

"Were Jack and Deirdre a couple?" Suddenly, Josie eyed an opener to unravel the mysterious secret Jack had kept about Deirdre.

"No, but Jack sure was in love with her. We all were at some point, I guess. She was the girl all the girls wanted to be and all the boys wanted to be with. But I can't recall she ever was in a relationship with anyone."

Ernie flipped on to the next page, which looked more like a family gathering, so Ernie just flipped past it.

"That's Ann. She must have been twelve at the time." Ernie pointed at a tiny girl in a picture taken inside the Salvation Army hall. The hall looked exactly the same as it did today.

"That was, of course, before I started looking after her."

Ernie flipped on.

"This is Jack and Jonathan outside Frank's. Jack was so proud when he started working there. Having his own job was really something. He was always proud of working at the hardware store."

They looked through two more albums and covered the eighties and the nineties, but as Ernie got married and they had children, the pictures of Jack or anyone else outside the family, for that matter, became scarcer. After looking through a half album of nothing but Ann and the children, Josie reckoned she had seen all the pictures he had with Jack in.

"Thanks so much for your help," Josie said and finished her tea.

"No problem. I hope it was at least some help," he said as he got up from his chair.

"Just sit. I'll see myself out."

"Oh, I need to move my legs a bit," he said, limping after her. "It takes some steps before my hips agree to walk along with me."

Josie walked slowly so that Ernie could follow before he got up to speed.

"So are you going to meet the new DC in Seattle on Friday?"

"I'm not sure. It depends how much I manage to prepare for the funeral."

"I think it will be good for you to get a change of scenery before the funeral," he said and tapped her shoulder before she stepped out the door.

# Chapter 12

Josie was still buttoning her jacket as she got out on the main street. The smell of smoke lay in the air as a constant reminder of the fire. Josie thought she could drop by the hardware store, number one on Ernie's list, while she was out and about. It was a slow day at the hardware store. It was a slow day on any account in Kayne, a small town not used to disasters of any kind, to see someone they knew and loved being swept away by a fire. Of course, still, on a sad day, you'd need to eat something, so the grocery store and even the diner had some customers. But at Frank's, there had hardly been anyone inside the doors. Jonathan had sent Lissie home and was alone in the store when Josie dropped by.

"Slow day?"

"Tell me about it," Jonathan answered. "I had some jobs in my book for today, but it felt wrong dropping by to change locks or repair heating systems on a day like this." Jonathan sat on a stool behind the counter and was tipping back and forth on it as Josie came in.

"Is there anything I can do for you?"

"I'm afraid I'm a poor customer today, but I hoped I could ask you some questions."

"About what?"

Josie explained to him about her preparations for the funeral. Jonathan didn't mind. It was not like it interfered with some business as she was the only one in the store.

"Sure, maybe I was among the ones who were close to him, but sometimes I wonder if anyone at all was close to him."

"What do you mean?"

"He would say 'mornin'' when he came in and 'bye' when he left. Sometimes that was all he said during a day. It was like he was in his own bubble. But by all means, a good man."

## LIKE SMOKE IN THE WIND

The door opened and Ms. Jensen popped in. Jonathan got up from the chair and straightened his back.

"How may I help you, miss?"

"Smoke detectors; mine are old and I fear they are broken," she said as she removed the gloves from her hands. Josie assumed she came straight from Ashville and her school there. "I've been putting it off for some time, but with all that's happened, I said to myself that it needed fixing today."

"Sure, how many do you need?" Jonathan said and moved over to the aisle where he kept all the home security.

"I'm not sure."

"These three talk together. If one goes off, they will all go off." He pulled a three-pack of smoke detectors down from the shelf.

She thanked him and paid and soon Jonathan and Josie were left to themselves again.

"You and Jack were about the same age, weren't you?" she asked, to get back into the conversation. She thought maybe he could say more about him while he was young.

"He was a year older than me, so he started working here full time when I was in my senior year."

"I've heard about that infamous senior year," she said, recalling Peggy's rant at the diner and the conversations from the home league.

"Infamous?"

"The boys making a top five list of the girls in the school."

"Sure." He shook his head. "It was quite innocent until Oscar came and made us make a bet about who could sleep with the most girls on the list." He shook his head. It wasn't his proudest moment. "This appalled Jack from the beginning. He was like: if I can't get Deirdre, then I don't want anyone. And of course he couldn't have Deirdre either."

"And you?"

"I was young and foolish, so at first I thought it was quite cool, but then I fell in love with Lissie. Of course, I didn't want everyone else to go after Lissie. So I talked to Oscar and said, 'Hey, let's drop this. I'm with Lissie now.'"

"So, how did he respond to that?"

"He said Lissie wasn't on the list, but Peggy was. That was only nonsense. Peggy was nowhere near the list, but she would be considered an easy point."

55

"Okay." Josie wasn't quite aware of how to comment on allegations like that.

"Everyone thought I didn't like Oscar because he pulled Lissie from the list, but that didn't bother me."

"Then what was it?"

"He was a jerk, that's all." He said it like it was a straight-out fact that everybody knew. Josie's impression at the time was that everybody was either highly impressed by him, or they thought he was a jerk. "I remember it clearly. It was on the day Lissie became a soldier. I was sitting beside Oscar that day. I told him we should drop the whole top-five thing. He said why, I just scored two points last night. Then he removed Lissie from the list, but all that had nothing to do with it. It was later in the meeting." Jonathan was looking out in the air. "Remember it like yesterday. Deirdre was playing the piano, and she played wrong. She never did that. Maybe some small error that we wouldn't hear, but this was an obvious mistake. Then I looked at Oscar and he was laughing, not loud, but I could clearly see he was laughing." Jonathan shook his head. The behavior still caused him dismay. "She was his cousin. He lived together with her and her family and he sat there laughing at her mistake."

Jonathan got up and started arranging the padlocks that hung near the counter. It already seemed to be in perfect order as far as she could see. Every one sorted by its brand. In fact, the entire store was in immaculate order. Still, Jonathan moved them around, placing the smaller ones at the top and the larger ones at the bottom. Josie guessed it was all about changing topic of the conversation. Josie didn't mind; it had all derailed from the talk about Jack anyway.

"I actually got closer to Jack after that. I wasn't hanging with Oscar and the other guys, so I started hanging out with Jack instead." Jonathan looked away from the shelves for a moment. "Didn't talk much back then either, but as trustworthy a person there ever was."

# Chapter 13

"We're pretty much done here," he said, standing on the stairs of the Salvation Army with his large cowboy hat in his hands. He looked super awkward, like he was about to propose or something.

"And I thought that... that..." he continued, no less awkward. "You have been super helpful, so I thought, maybe I could buy you a lunch as a thank you?" He had drawn his breath and gone for it.

"Like, right now?"

"Sure, going back to Spokane today, so..."

"Okay, but only if you leave the hat behind," she said with a tease.

"What's wrong with my hat?" Fred had exclaimed as he looked at it.

He had left the hat behind, and they had gone to the diner. After all, the diner was the only place to go. They had found a booth back in the corner near the restrooms to get some kind of privacy. Still, she knew this would spin off so many rumors that she would never see the end of.

"So the investigation is over?" Josie said for no other reason than to make conversation.

"Sure, it's basically a routine thing. Unless the conclusion of the fire investigators should say anything else, we conclude it's an accident."

"The accident we feared for some time, that stubborn fool," Josie replied.

"Or you can look at it this way. He got to live in his house until he died, and that's what he wanted," he replied.

"Maybe you're right."

"Now tell me, what does an officer in the Salvation Army do in Kayne?"

"A little bit of everything. Part minister, part social worker and even part detective."

"Detective as well. I'm intrigued, do tell."

She didn't get around to telling anything before Peggy showed up to take their order.

"Would you like to order something?" she said and smiled an overly cute smile as if she was interrupting two teenagers' first date. Josie considered if she should say anything, but guessed it would be useless anyway. Her potential love life was one of the hottest topics of gossip in town. Especially after someone found out that an officer no longer needed to marry another officer, which had been a longstanding rule in the army. Sometimes Josie thought things would be easier if that rule still applied.

"Well, I'd like a good burger if that's on your menu."

"Sure." Peggy smiled.

"No," Josie broke in. "We'll take the special lunch for today, both of us."

Fred gave her a bewildered look. He wasn't used to ladies ordering his food, and he was not sure how he felt about it.

"Anything to drink?" Peggy wasn't sure whom to address anymore.

"Water, sparkling for me," Josie said.

"I'll take that too," Fred replied. Peggy nodded and was on her way surprisingly fast. Josie reckoned she had news to spread.

"And what's the special lunch?" Fred asked.

"I don't know. Just trust me, it's better than the burgers."

"Ah," Fred said and nodded. "So, what's your ongoing investigation?" He tapped his fingers on the table and looked at Josie with anticipation.

"I hoped you would leave it."

"Leave a piece of info like that, not a chance."

"Okay," she said. "This town is divided because of two very influential men that used to be best friends, but for the past forty or so years have hated each other. If the town shall move on, they need to resolve this argument. And if I'm going to help them do this, I need to find out what really happened."

"That sounds like a tough case," Fred said.

"Luckily, my evidence doesn't need to be as solid as what you search for."

"You don't think this will end up in court?"

"No, I really hope not," Josie said.

"Hello, Lieutenant." Old Bella approached them.

"Hello, Bella," Josie said and waited for Bella to say something more. But Bella just stood before them with both hands, holding her purse in front of her. "How are you?" Josie continued.

## LIKE SMOKE IN THE WIND

"I'm fine," she answered. Then she stood there and smiled, first to Josie, then to Fred, and then back again. But she said nothing more.

"Bella," Josie said. "The bathrooms are over there." Josie pointed at the restroom doors.

"Oh, that's right," Bella replied. "You'll have to excuse me, but I was on my way to the bathroom." Bella smiled and disappeared. Fred looked baffled at Josie, but Josie acted like nothing out of the ordinary had happened.

"But your investigation," Fred said when he had finally processed the latest encounter with the locals. "Do you have any clues so far?"

"The daughter of one of them died in a fire at a mill in the late seventies."

"And there's a connection there?"

"That's when they started falling out, so I guess so."

"Could be, and then again, it could not." Fred smiled, clearly enjoying Josie's investigating attempts.

"And there's something off about her. Her father didn't have a single photo of her in his living room. And no one talks about her, ever. I only accidentally heard about her because Jack Sutton, who was very demented, mistook me for her."

"So she looked like you?"

"Not at all," she said, remembering the teenager from Ernie's photo album. "But he mistook me for a lot of women and none of them really looked like me."

"No one here really looks like you," Fred replied. "That was meant as a compliment," he added after a brief pause.

"Thanks," she said. She was most grateful that he delivered the compliment in a way that wasn't cheesy or pushy. Peggy rounded the corner with the food. It was a pasta dish that was today's lunch. Josie had tasted this one before, not that it was a genuine Italian cuisine, but it tasted rather well. Peggy placed the plates in front of them, and glasses and water bottles beside that. Then she just stood there and looked at them. Fred froze like he was in the middle of a ritual he didn't understand.

"Thank you, Peggy," Josie said. Peggy smiled and moved away.

"What was that all about?"

"Peggy is Peggy," Josie said, and didn't really know what more to say about it.

"Really, tell me, how is it to live in a small town?"

"You tell me, Mr. Spokane." Josie opened her bottle and waited for it to fizz out before she poured some in her glass.

"Spokane is, in fact, the second largest town in Washington."

"My point exactly. Now get yourself something to eat," she said and lifted her fork in the air.

"Fair enough," Fred said. "I don't like pasta."

"Then you'll drive hungry back to Spokane."

"Actually, I love pasta," he said with a smile. "I just wanted to guilt you for hijacking my order."

"Trust me, I saved you."

"Well, I have no choice but to trust you on this, I guess."

"It has its up and downs."

"What has – the burgers?"

"No living in a small city," Josie said. "I miss the big city vibe sometimes. The job sometimes takes me to Spokane or Seattle, and of course I sometimes visit my family back in LA. Then I try to soak up as much of the big city as I can."

Fred just nodded, engulfed in his pasta.

"But on the other hand, here everyone knows who the lieutenant at the Salvation Army is," she said, trying hard to mimic the broad dialect the old ones in Kayne had.

"Sure, being at the center of all gossip and so," Fred said, and laughed. They verified the truth of the statement as they later walked out of the diner and back to the Salvation Army where he had parked his car. The number of eyes staring out at them gave a clear indication that more than a few had been waiting for them to pass. Fred walked casually, as if he had no worries in the world. Easy for him. He was going back to Spokane. Josie had buried her hands in her pocket and kept the right distance. Too far off would make Fred feel she avoided him. She felt that would be rude to the man that had just bought her lunch. Besides, she liked him. He was a nice fellow. Then she couldn't move close enough that all the onlookers would view them as a couple.

"Thank you for lunch," she said as they finally arrived outside the army.

"My pleasure," he replied. "I'm not kidding. You really helped us out."

Josie smiled. "You're welcome."

## LIKE SMOKE IN THE WIND

Fred dug into his pockets for the car keys, and a second later, the mechanical sound of locks opening sounded from the Ford. Fred opened the door and put one foot inside before he turned toward Josie.

"Call me next time you're in Spokane to soak in the vibe," he said and smiled. "I'd love to hear how the investigation goes."

"Sure, I'll do that," Josie said and nodded.

Fred stepped inside, and soon he was on his way back to Spokane.

# Chapter 14

"Hello, come right on in," Marge said as she opened the door. Josie passed her and walked on to the living room with Marge on her tail. "I would offer you something to eat, but I hear you just had lunch with the detective."

"How could you possibly know that? It was literally two minutes ago."

"Rumors travel fast."

"But really, that fast?"

"Before the phone came to Kayne, someone would run and tell everyone. Now, with phones, everything is so much easier." Marge chuckled.

Josie sighed and shook her head.

"But he seems nice, though, the inspector?"

"Come on, Marge, not you too..."

"No, no, I was just saying...I guess you're here to plan the reception after the funeral," she said.

Josie had just learned about this Kayne tradition that when someone died, the community got together and made the reception. The upside of this was, of course, that when someone like Jack died, Carl wouldn't sit alone with all the details around the funeral. Heaven knows if there would have been a reception after the funeral at all. And Jack deserved it. The other upside was the food. With all homemade sandwiches and cakes, it tasted a lot better than any catering company delivering to funerals. Josie already knew this because she had tasted the Kayne baking on several other occasions. The flip side was that everyone waited for the Salvation Army officer to ask. Luckily, Marge knew this backwards and forwards. "Yes," Josie said. She guessed it was obvious. Marge often helped her to plan practical things.

"I talked to Ernie yesterday," Marge said.

"I get it, you talk."

"I'll tell you whom to talk to, but I'm afraid that only the officer at the Salvation Army is good enough to make the actual request," Marge said, and

## LIKE SMOKE IN THE WIND

chuckled. "I'm afraid that someone would be terribly disappointed if I called them."

"If someone else could have done it, I wouldn't ask you anyway."

"Why not?" she said with a confused slash insulted expression.

"I'd ask Peggy, and everyone would've been informed in a heartbeat."

Marge laughed, albeit a bit guilt-ridden. She was not sure if the joke was appropriate, but since it came from the officer, it sort of had to be.

Marge gave Josie a long list of people to call to ask favors from for the reception later on. Everyone easily agreed, and some would probably be insulted for not being asked as well. Food was the simple task. It provided them a chance to show off their new cake recipe or their latest inspiration for sandwiches. But the whole ordeal also meant a lot of practical arrangements. They had to use the Salvation Army hall for the reception, only hours after the same hall was used for the funeral. This meant that chairs needed to be removed and tables to be set in, and it needed to be decorated. Marge said that she and Ann could arrange the tablecloth and decoration. But she needed some men to set up tables before they could do that. This, Marge had warned, was not an equally popular task as preparing the food.

Of course, it was different, while the ladies could wait until the last moment, and then march in with their cake for all to see which cake they had baked. The men moving chairs would need to rush back from the grave and fix the tables in a hurry before the others came back. No one would know who did it, and let's face it, no one compliments you for putting tables in a straight line. So the practical jobs were harder to find volunteers for. So while they arranged the food-list during a half an hour of calls, getting the men to show up, she decided to do face to face. She tracked through Marge's backyard to shortcut into Silver Lake Road. She wouldn't think of doing this if it hadn't been that Marge constantly insisted on her doing just that. Her first stop was Oscar. He lived in the Harriett House. Same as the stores were named after people who owned them years ago, the houses were named after people who'd lived there ages ago. Josie had no idea who this Harriett was, and neither had Oscar. She had asked him once.

The wind made a sizzling sound in the spruces that lined up on each side of the street. The Harriett House was a small house, almost like a cottage. She was told it once had a marvelous garden, with rose trees, lilacs, and lilies all

63

over. Oscar had removed anything from the garden that would be considered time-consuming and was left with a tiny lawn behind a white picket fence. The house was one of the reasons Josie couldn't quite see the family connection with George and Jerry. They lived in the largest house in Kayne, and this was among the smallest. From the gate to the front door, there were only a few steps. She had to ring the doorbell three times and feared she'd missed him when he finally opened the door.

"Ah, our young and beautiful Lieutenant Josie. Please step inside my humble abode." He waved her in like a music conductor.

*Sure, whatever,* Josie thought and tried to hide a sigh.

"You still don't drink coffee, do you?"

"No."

"Well, can I offer you some pop?"

This attitude toward her was common, and it was code for: you don't drink coffee yet, so you are not yet an adult. Once you grow up, of course you will drink coffee. And offering soda was the confirmation. *Will you accept the children's drink I'm offering you?*

"A glass of cold water will be fine," Josie answered. She would never give them the satisfaction.

"Now, what can I do for you?" he said as he entered with a glass of water.

Josie explained about the funeral and asked him to help her out by putting up tables in the hall for the reception.

"Hmm," he said, and scratched his chin. "Well."

"You are going to the funeral?"

"Yes, sure I am."

"And you will come to the reception after?"

"Sure," he said, and she immediately knew she had trapped him. What kind of excuse for being busy could he possibly come up with if he already had set this day apart for the funeral? "Who else is helping out?"

"Jerry and Hoss." She thought of mentioning Jonathan, but realized that could easily backfire.

"Of course, it's the least I can do for an old friend."

"You and Jack were close?"

"Sure, well, everyone in Kayne is close and I guess we weren't the ones who were closest."

## LIKE SMOKE IN THE WIND

"Why not? You're the same age, aren't you?"

"Yes, of course. This may sound silly, but he had a major crush on Deirdre. You know, Uncle George's girl. I lived there at the time, so she was almost like a sister to me. Boys are obligated to resent the boys that come after his sister." He chuckled to soften the dislike part. "Nothing big, of course, but we didn't bond in the same way, that's all."

"So you and Deirdre were close?"

"Sure, we were sometimes very close, I'd say." Oscar switched position in his chair and pulled his hand through his hair. "Of course we had our quarrels as well, but who hasn't?" He giggled. Oscar sat on the edge of his chair and slightly twisted his upper body while he stared blankly into the air. No, that wasn't it; he was more arranging his head in the right position. Like it was something he had rehearsed in front of the mirror, but couldn't quite recreate. *Is he posing for me?* Josie thought. An involuntary grin appeared on her face at the thought of what an almost seventy-year-old man hoped to achieve by posing for a woman in her twenties.

"Well, I have to get going. I need to talk to Jerry and Hoss also this evening," she said, and got up from her chair to emphasize her haste.

"Jerry and Hoss? I thought you said they were in already?"

"They will be. Don't worry."

"Oh, you're a sneaky one," Oscar replied. Josie just smiled back and thanked him for the water and the promised help.

# Chapter 15

"Good morning, Josie, breakfast is ready." Major Hattie stood in the doorway and the light poured in to the bedroom, forcing Josie to rub her eyes. She could smell the fresh brewed coffee and hoped tea was a part of the breakfast as well.

"We'll eat and plan the day." The old major gave Josie a warm smile that Josie tried to return but was too dozy to pull off. The door closed, and the room went dark again. Josie lay back on her pillow and curled the duvet into her arms. What to do? The question kept ringing in her ears.

Every once in a while she, along with the other officers in the division, met in Seattle. This time, it had been the installment of the new Divisional Commander. She had come to the meeting on Friday evening, and stayed over at the secretary at the DHQ, Major Hattie. Josie treasured these trips and always tried to put in an extra day or two to feel the city life before returning to Kayne. Then she would do all the things she missed in Kayne. Drinking tea at a coffee shop, shopping for clothes or going to the movies. But now there was one thing that she wanted more than ever. She was curious about Deirdre. She had applied to the training college, so there had to be a file on her here at the DHQ. But she didn't know if she could just ask to see it.

Josie came to the breakfast table in her PJs without doing anything but washing her face. From Claire Hattie's breakfast table, she had a view over the Seattle skyline with the Space Needle at its center. But what Josie loved about the view lay beyond the skyline, the Pacific. They couldn't see the ocean anywhere near Kayne, and she missed that. She stood and admired the view that now was bathing in sunshine, when she was interrupted by Claire.

"Come and have some breakfast before it gets cold."

Claire had made pancakes for breakfast. The first time they met was at the congress in LA last year when Josie had received her first order ever, going to Kayne. Hattie had been furious that they sent a young woman all alone to such a desolate place. She had done her share of orders in no-man's-land, and knew how lonely it could be. They had agreed that Josie could visit her in Seattle

# LIKE SMOKE IN THE WIND

whenever she needed. Even though they were forty years apart in both age and years of service, they had become close friends.

"You're totally spoiling me," Josie said as she sat down.

"I thought you needed some spoiling right now, with a funeral at hand and everything."

Josie just nodded as she dug into the first pancake.

"One thing is the funerals when people die of old age in their bed. But when the death is caused by something as tragic as a fire, that is something entirely different."

Josie nodded. It had been much harder to make people talk about it, and especially Carl, who was drowning every bad memory in booze.

"Tea?" Claire said as she moved around the table to Josie's side with her old tea pot. She had inherited it from an aunt and was really proud of it. Claire was more of a coffee drinker, so she only got to use the pot when she had tea-drinking guests.

"Yes, please," Josie replied. She didn't need to ask what kind of tea it was. She already knew. The tea pot was an old Sadler pot, a proper English tea pot that also needed proper English tea. Josie didn't mind. In fact, she preferred some plain black tea, at least for breakfast, but she wasn't sure every guest of Claire viewed it similarly.

"Well, today, let's set our minds on other things than your problems up in Kayne. What shall we do?"

"I'm afraid I can't entirely forget about Kayne today. First, I need a suit." Josie had gone on explaining about Carl, and how he had really nothing to wear at the funeral.

"Okay, let's check the thrift store on Aurora Street. I know the manager there. What is the second point?"

"There is a girl from Kayne that died in a fire. She was supposed to go to the training college, so I guess you've got a copy of her papers in your archives."

"When was that?" Claire said, more like a question to her own memory. "Sometime in the seventies, I thought I heard of something like that. What's her name?"

"Deirdre Chisholm."

"Yes, there was a lot of talk about it, an awful tragedy."

Josie just nodded.

"Let's see if we can round up the suit first, and then we can go to the DHQ and see if there still are any papers left. I can't promise anything, though."

"Thanks," Josie said and nodded.

"But first you've got to eat your breakfast."

They had found a dark gray almost black suit that looked nearly brand new and should fit nicely. They might have to shorten the legs, but there were enough handy women in Kayne who could fix that in no time. From there, they went straight to the DHQ. It was on the ground floor of an office building on Queen Anne Avenue, close to the Elliott bay. The DHQ was usually closed on Saturdays, so Claire had to lock herself in.

"That's my desk," she said, and pointed to the desk in the reception area. Further in, the DCs had their offices, but Claire took Josie even further in beyond the restrooms.

"It's the storage room, and it's basically a mess," she said as she put the key in the lock. "When we moved from the old offices to this place, we just placed the old filing cabinets in here. I guess this is where it is, if we still got it."

The mess statement was not an exaggeration. It was old office furniture, some army flags, a few red kettles, and everything with thick layers of dust on it. Claire moved a few chairs to get over to the far wall where they had two old gray filing cabinets. They both had their key in them. The files were sorted by topic. Every corps had its own file. She pulled the Kayne file and handed it to Josie.

"Check if there's something there."

Josie opened the file. It contained blueprints of the hall, something about the hundred years anniversary and some correspondence between the corps leaders and DC, but nothing on Deirdre.

"No, nothing here." Josie handed her the file.

Claire placed it back where she found it and opened the second one.

"Hmm, this might be something," she said. "What's her name again?"

"Deirdre - Deirdre Chisholm."

"That's c." Claire scrolled over the files with her index finger. "Chisholm, here it is."

## LIKE SMOKE IN THE WIND

Claire pulled out a file and handed it to Josie.

"Let's go to my desk and look at it in a brighter and less dusty place," Claire suggested.

"Good idea," Josie said, already feeling the dust tickling in her nose.

Josie sat down on Claire's chair while Claire found herself another chair. She pulled out the papers and laid them upside down, so she could read them from the oldest to the newest. She, of course, expected the latter ones to be most interesting, but she wanted the whole story. First off was the application to the training college. Josie flipped through it and realized it had changed quite a bit in half a century. Still, she didn't read it. It was basically a bunch of yesses and no's to a ton of questions. Then there was the recommendation from the corps' leader. Josie read it. It was one type-written page, with mostly what one could expect. She was active in the corps, played piano at the meetings, helped as a teen leader and was a good example amongst the young people in the corps. It ended with a warm recommendation from a Captain Todd Jensen. Josie assumed that would be the husband of the Jensen Jack sometimes mistook her for. Behind that was the recommendation from the DC. It was a brief statement that he gave his recommendations. The last piece of paper was a handwritten note from Deirdre herself.

'I am extremely grateful that I have been accepted to the training college. I am also very regretful to announce that I have to withdraw my application due to personal reasons.

- yours sincerely, D Chisholm.'

"This can't be. Everyone told me she was going to the training college."

"Let me see," Claire said and took the paper and held it up toward the light. "It's dated April thirteen."

"That's only weeks before she died."

"That could be the explanation. Maybe she didn't get around to tell anyone," Claire said. "The Salvation Army would rather let her be remembered as the girl who died before going to training college rather than starting any speculation."

"That could make sense." Josie looked at the letter as Claire was still holding it up against the light. "Are those tears?" She pointed at two round, hardly visible spots at the bottom of the paper.

"It looks like it. After all, it wasn't a simple decision she made."

69

Claire laid the paper back on top of the others.

"What could be the personal reason?"

"From my experience back then, it was mainly one reason for girls and another one for the boys. For girls, it was becoming pregnant, and for the boys, it was that they couldn't stop smoking."

"Pregnant, really?"

"It's all speculation, of course, but 'personal' is often code for something you don't want to say."

Josie nodded. It made sense, and somehow it could make sense with other things she had heard about Deirdre, even though she'd disliked the gossipers ever being right. She folded the file together.

"It's lovely weather outside. What if we go to the sculpture park, and maybe grab a cup of tea and something to eat to bring along?"

"Sure, that sounds like a good idea."

They had stopped by a café and bought a cup of tea for Josie, a coffee for Claire, and some croissants on the way. They found a bench overlooking the ocean behind a large sculpture that looked like something from the *Transformers'* movies.

"Croissants is something I prefer eating outside. They are messy," Claire said.

"And it makes the birds happy."

"It is so precious with these last warm sunny days before the fall really sets in."

"I'm happy just looking at the ocean again," Josie said and took another bite of the croissant, making a dozen small crumbs fall to the ground.

"Not much of that up in the mountains."

"Hm-m," Josie replied, still chewing. "By the way, wouldn't the boys have sorted out their smoking issues when they became soldiers?"

"What boys?"

"The ones who withdrew their applications back in the seventies."

"Oh, you're still there. You need to let the Army be the Army for just one day. This is a day off, remember?"

## LIKE SMOKE IN THE WIND

"Sorry, that was the last question, I promise."

"Back then, the smoking ban was only for officers and important positions in the corps, like sergeant major and band master. The smoking ban for all soldiers came in seventy-eight."

Josie nodded, but had to agree with her, and the ocean view was more important right now.

"We were viewed as a strange cult when we banned smoking back then, but now smoking is banned almost everywhere."

"Told you so, world," Josie replied and took a long sip of her tea.

# Chapter 16

Jerry insisted on driving, and since Josie had driven all the way from Seattle last night, she was more than okay with that. It was around ten in the morning when Jerry's car took off to the narrow driveway that led to Carl's beat-up old cabin. The Salvation Army had dedicated the evening service to Jack as a memorial, and the goal would be that Carl should be there. The problem was that Carl had been drinking heavily the past few days. This was also a test. Tuesday at the funeral, he had to be sober. They had agreed to follow him closely until then. Both Jonathan and Jerry had volunteered to help Josie out. She liked it, that two of the most respected men in the community volunteered to help the local drunkie.

Carl's house, and Carl, was like she had seen it on Wednesday morning. The house was a mess, and so was Carl. A strong scent of cheap liquor slammed their faces as they entered. The tables with unfinished projects were the same as last time. His chair was the only change. Empty bottles were stacked around his chair even thicker than last time, and one bottle half filled with a brownish liquid stood on his table. On top of the plate with oatmeal Josie had fixed for him on Wednesday, three more plates were stacked. It looked like half of the food was still on the plates. Carl had hardly eaten.

"I don't take visitors today," Carl said.

"This is the tough day, Carl," Josie said. "Because now you need to sober up."

"Why?" he moaned.

"Because tonight is the memorial for Jack at the Salvation Army."

"And because you need to rehearse walking straight before the funeral on Tuesday," Jerry broke in.

"Jerry, is that you?"

"Sure is, old friend."

"I'll fix you some coffee and some food," Josie said and took the used plates into the kitchen. She suspected correctly that he wouldn't have much food

# LIKE SMOKE IN THE WIND

in the house, so she had brought some. She put on coffee first, the strong type. Then the frying pan needed washing to fry him some eggs and sausages. Luckily, he hadn't made too much of a mess in the kitchen since last she was there. He hardly had been in here except for the times he made whatever was on the plates she brought in from the living room.

"No, no, I need that one," Carl was complaining back in the living room. She assumed Jerry had collected all the liquor he had.

"So you're good cop and I'm bad cop today," Jerry said as he came in and emptied the booze into the kitchen sink.

"It's what they in Hollywood call 'character casting,'" she replied with a smile.

"Maybe I should wait for him to get busy eating before I search for the rest of the bottles," he said, watching the sausages frying in the pan.

"Sure, you can give him some coffee in the meantime." Josie found a mug and washed it under flowing hot water, and handed it to Jerry. The coffee maker had just about produced a cup of coffee. Jerry filled up the cup and placed the pot back in.

"Be careful, it's hot," Jerry warned Carl.

"Can I just have a little something in the cup?" Carl pleaded.

"If by a little something you mean cream, then sure."

"I don't use cream in my coffee." Carl made spitting sounds.

"Well then, no."

By the time Josie came with the food, Carl had to settle for plain black coffee.

"You should eat something."

"But I'm not hungry." Carl said.

"You never are, but this will do you good."

"It looks kinda good, though."

Josie sat down on a stool in front of him with the plate in her lap and steadied his hand, and helped him hold on to the fork as he ate. Jerry removed the empty bottles. Josie could hear that he was checking the kitchen cabinets, and every once in a while, she heard the sound of a bottle being emptied into the sink. After a while, he came back into the living room and started searching through the cabinets there.

"That's not necessary," Carl objected.

## ISAAC LIND

"I'm afraid it is, Carl," Josie said. "We need you to be sober at the funeral."

"I shouldn't go to the funeral."

"You're his only relative. You must go."

"But I let him down. I don't deserve to go."

"Jack loved you," Josie said and looked him straight in his eyes.

"I let everybody down," he said and started crying. Josie held him. His head fell down on her shoulder and she could feel the wet tears on her neck. Jerry kept walking back and forth between the living room and the kitchen.

"You must eat some more." Josie helped Carl to straighten up so he could get some more food and coffee. "When you are done, you need to take a bath."

"Why?" he protested once again.

"I have a suit for you. One for you to wear on Tuesday, but I can't let you try it on as dirty as you are now," she said. "Besides, we need you to look clean tonight."

Carl had no bathroom in his cabin for bathing. He had a huge tin bath tub they placed in the middle of the living room and filled it with water. They needed to fill up buckets in the kitchen and take it in to the living room. Josie had brought new underwear and clean towels. She helped him unbutton his shirt.

"Now you clean up, and we will wait outside."

Carl nodded. They both went into the kitchen and Josie finished up the dishes. They could hear Carl struggling with his clothes, and at one point, it sounded like he was about to tumble over. But soon after, they heard him in the water making gentle splashing sounds. He was done, almost at the same time that she was done with the dishes. When he called them out, he was smiling, clean and in new underwear, but undoubtfully still drunk. Jerry emptied the tub the same way he had filled it up, using a bucket. Josie helped Carl get into the suit she got in Seattle. He smiled as he viewed himself in the mirror.

"It's like I'm getting married," he said.

"That would be something," Josie said. "I see we need to shorten the arms and legs, but just a bit. Just stand still and I'll put in some pins."

Carl held his arms straight forward and Josie folded them carefully and put in some pins to hold them in place. Then she folded up one leg and put some pins in them.

"Aaauoch, I am standing still, but you're sticking me anyway," Carl shouted.

74

## LIKE SMOKE IN THE WIND

"I'm sorry," Josie said, struggling not to laugh at him.

"I'm not sure that I like this suit," he said when he had taken it off and was getting into ordinary clothes.

"I promise, next time you wear this, it will have no pins in it," Josie said. "I'll find you another cup of coffee."

When she came back in from the kitchen with a fresh cup of coffee, he was back in his chair.

"Here, take this." His hands were steady enough to hold the cup by himself. Jerry came back after moving the tub where it used to be stored.

"Jerry was my best friend," Carl said.

"Really?"

"Back in school, we were best buds," Carl said and breathed between every word. "But I disappointed him so terribly."

"No, you didn't," Jerry replied.

"I was so... There was this old mill, you know."

"The one that burned down?" Josie said.

"Yes, that's the one... I did something terrible." Carl looked down and hid his face in his hands.

"We have talked about this before," Jerry said, and got down on one knee before him and whispered into his ear.

"I know..." Carl said.

"I have told you this. That is nothing for you to think about. No one is blaming you." Jerry sounded almost scary, a threat in his voice as he said it. Carl just nodded.

"But all the things that I did?"

"Don't worry about it."

Carl did worry, because he was sobbing for several minutes after.

"We need to go now, but I'll come and pick you up later for the meeting. Okay?" Josie said.

Carl nodded.

"Now you try to get some rest."

Carl continued to nod as Josie and Jerry left the cabin.

"Everything is so dark when he is sobering up," Jerry said as they walked to the car.

# Chapter 17

The Army flag in the hall was decorated by a white ribbon; apart from that, everything was as normal. At least on the outside. Normally, this would be a regular Sunday sermon, but today there was the mentioning of Jack's passing and a prayer for his family. The brutal circumstances of his death colored the atmosphere and everyone knew that this meeting would all be centered around his tragic passing. Josie's hopes of having Carl in the meeting had backfired. As a part of his sobering up, he had vomited all afternoon. When she came to bring him to the meeting, she had to help him get washed and clean up around the chair, and get in him something to drink to avoid dehydration. Finally she had helped him to bed. She thought she had plenty of time for getting him dressed and driving down to the Army. She had not bargained for all that work, but she couldn't just leave him like that. She went to her car and found an apron she had brought just in case, and started washing.

At one point, it was obvious that she would not reach the meeting on time. She had called Ernie and told him to begin without her. She hadn't left until she was sure Carl was in a state that it was okay to leave him. Arriving back at the Army, she was smelling of vomit and moonshine. Josie snuck up to her apartment and took a fast shower before she came down in the middle of the meeting, passing the aisles and up to the platform as they sang the last song before her sermon as if it was all part of the plan. Someone would surely talk of how irresponsible it was of the young lieutenant to come this late into such an important meeting. And because of the confidentiality, she could not explain why she was late. There was nothing to do about it but to rise above it. She held her talk, and they had given people a chance to light a candle for Jack. Now the mercy seat was filled with shining lights.

They served coffee and some cakes after the meeting. Most people stayed behind. They had some tables in the second hall, but most people found a place to sit in the rows, balancing their coffee and cakes in their hands. George and Frank kept an eye on each other, and when George got a spot at one table in the

# LIKE SMOKE IN THE WIND

second hall, Frank decided to leave. Jonathan left with him, but Lissie stayed behind.

Josie passed the crowd in the second hall and entered the kitchen.

"Is all good here?"

"No, I can't find my army keys anywhere," Marge said. Marge had two key chains, one for her private keys, and one for the keys to the Salvation Army. She and Ernie were the only two people that, in addition to the keys to the main door as many people had, also had the keys to the office and to Josie's apartment.

"Are you sure you brought them?"

"I thought I did."

"I am sure they'll show up somewhere, either here or at home." Josie smiled her most reassuring smile.

"You're probably right."

"I meant to ask if you needed any help here."

"No, no, you just go and chat with everybody."

Josie went back into the hall. There were no available seats by the tables, so she continued to the main hall, where she noticed Ms. Jensen. Oscar Bowers had sat down beside her and was more or less leaning over her. Ms. Jensen was a quite charming single woman in her late forties. Oscar Bowers considered himself to be a divine gift to all the single ladies in the world. He had, in the beginning, tried out a flirty tone with Josie, something she usually shot down quite brutally. Ms. Jensen, however, was afraid to hurt anyone's feelings, so she never really turned him down. This made him believe he had more of a chance than he really had. Josie returned to the kitchen and got a cup of tea and a cup of coffee before she got back into the hall.

"Ms. Jensen, could you help me with something?" Josie said and pointed toward the piano.

"Sure," she answered. She turned to Oscar Bowers. "Excuse me, but I need to help the lieutenant for a moment."

"No problem. I'll make sure no one takes your place."

Ms. Jensen gave him a smile that best could be described as a 'Pan-am-smile.'

"You know you can trust me, my sweet little biscuit." Oscar leaned back as if he had the girl all lined up. Ms. Jensen hurried after Josie up on the platform.

77

Josie walked over to the piano. She pulled a chair that she placed beside the stool and sat down. Ms. Jensen sat down on the stool.

"Now what can I help you with, Lieutenant?"

"Nothing," Josie said and handed her the cup of coffee.

"What, you just said you needed help, didn't you?"

"I lied. It looked like you needed a change of scenery."

Ms. Jensen looked at Oscar Bowers, who sat down in the hall and guarded Ms. Jensen's seat, and raised her eyebrows.

"He sure can be a handful."

"So tell it to him. You don't have to take all his crap."

"I can't just do that, can I?"

"Why not?" Josie said casually, as if it was the most normal thing in the world. Not that she didn't care if she hurt people; she just didn't care if she hurt people that behaved badly against her.

"Well, after what I've understood, he has been turned away by most women in Kayne by now."

"It's that bad, is it?"

Ms. Jensen just nodded.

"Just a tiny question about the small-town gossip. I heard he was quite popular in his youth. Why didn't he marry when all the other boys married?"

"I don't ever think he was that popular. Of course, he moved here from Seattle just before I was born or right after. I remember talk about him as a big city boy when I was a little girl." Ms. Jensen stopped and smiled.

"What is it?"

"I guess it's a hang-up we've got being such a small town. It was the same when you came to town, a young woman straight from LA. It's like we wanted to place you on a pedestal and display you for the entire world – look, we got a bit of L.A. and Hollywood and all that."

Josie laughed. She had noticed.

"But when that blew over, he was nothing special. And he was far from as popular as he would claim to be."

Ms. Jensen sat quietly and sipped her coffee for a while.

"Maybe that was the problem. Maybe the attention he got in the beginning went a bit to his head and he never quite recovered."

## LIKE SMOKE IN THE WIND

"I guess you'd better check if the piano is still in tune or something like that before he gets suspicious."

"Sure," she said and opened the lid to the keys. She was gently playing first the octaves up and down on the keyboard, and then some major chords. It was, of course, far too noisy for her to hear if the piano was still in tune, but Oscar wouldn't know that. Eventually, Oscar realized that Ms. Jensen wasn't returning and turned his attention elsewhere.

As people made ready to leave, Josie went down to the door and greeted everyone as they left. When the hall was empty, Marge and Ann were done in the kitchen.

"Found your keys yet?" Josie asked.

"No, I'm afraid they're nowhere to be found."

"Now you go home, and you can search for them at home when there's daylight."

"That's probably a good idea, but you need to lock the door after us then."

"Sure, that's not a problem. Have a good night, both of you." Josie followed the ladies up to the door. "Tell me if you can't find the key, so I can give you a spare."

# Chapter 18

Josie peeked out through the blinders of her bedroom window. The sun was about to rise, but the clear sky boded for a nice day.

"That's unfair," she told herself, knowing that most of this day she'd spend writing the sermon for tomorrow's funeral. She had no clue what to write. To be honest, she hadn't given the sermon as much thought as she felt she should. There had been so much else to occupy her mind. She semi-sleepwalked to the kitchen and filled the water boiler on pure reflex. No worries before the first cup of tea. The fridge also suffered from the fact that she had been preoccupied with other stuff. She had cereal, but not enough milk for more than half a bowl. The last remains of bread were dry and uneatable. She brought a cup of tea along with her to the bathroom. After a shower and a cup of tea, her spirits were slightly higher. It was still an hour and a half until the grocery store opened, so she had to make do with what she had.

She had some cheese and made a couple of unexciting pieces of toast. But it was easy to eat, and she could read up on Bible verses and take notes as she ate them. She had googled Bible verses and funerals, and went through a long list of verses to see if any one could be a starting point for a sermon. Some verses she immediately dismissed, like Isaiah fifty-seven verse one. 'The righteous perish, and no one takes it to heart.' There was probably much truth in it, but certainly not something Josie would ever say at a funeral. She also found a lot of good verses that she could use, but none gave her an idea about what to say. There was always someone who would tell her to wait for the inspiration, but with the funeral tomorrow, there were limits to how long she could wait. On the other hand, she had experienced that sometimes the Lord favored hard labor. And for Josie, writing sermons was indeed hard work. She needed to sweat her way through it and first, after it was done, the Lord would give her His approval. That it was her first funeral certainly didn't help the matter at hand. The worst part was that her head was so filled up with thoughts about all that had happened the last few days. She had learned the hard way that staring into the computer screen or the wallpaper, for that matter, never helped her. Fresh air and a walk just might. And it was the weather for it. The problem with a walk in Kayne was that it so often caused a lot of other distractions. She planned to go up the road past Jack's burnt down house and into one trail that circled Kayne. That way, she would run into the fewest people. At least, that was the plan.

The air was crisp and almost painful if she filled up her lungs too fast, but it was an extraordinarily bright morning. All the sounds were distant and the most prominent sound was of her stepping on the gravel at the side of the road. She had not walked far before she doubted her decision to go up the road. A fire truck was parked outside Jack's house and it had already gathered a crowd. As she came nearer, the firefighters were making their hoses ready, as if they expected it to start burning again.

"What's going on?" she asked Ernie, who was leaning his back to his fence, a bit away from the crowd.

"The house is dangerously close to collapsing, so they have decided to burn it down to the ground to make sure there are no accidents."

"Thanks," she replied before she made way through the crowd. She recognized Chief Henderson amongst the firefighters.

"Chief Henderson," she called out. The chief turned and smiled when he saw her. "I guess your investigation of the cause of fire is done."

"Yes, it was an electrical error in the hot water tank," he said before he bowed in toward Josie to talk a bit more privately. "Not so uncommon in these rural places. People are fixing everything themselves."

He straightened himself up before he continued. "In fact, it is the second most common reason for fires outside of Spokane."

"Is there anything of his stuff that was salvageable?" Josie thought it would be nice for Carl to have something to remember him by.

"No, nothing," he answered without hesitation. "Or... one firefighter said that the nightstand on his first-floor bedroom wasn't burnt down."

Josie thought of his second-floor bedroom. He hadn't used that in years. They had closed off the first floor for him when he became demented, to prevent any accident. And who knows, that might have given him a few extra years to live.

## ISAAC LIND

"You see, it was made of mahogany, a very hard wood, and being up on the second floor, it was reasonably intact. The nightstand itself is ruined, but if there were something in the drawer, it may have survived."

"Is it possible to get it out?"

"Sure, but don't keep your hopes too high," he said before he left her and addressed one of the other firefighters. The other firefighter went into the building as the others kept making preparations to burn the house to the ground.

It took about ten minutes before he came out with the drawer in his hands. The front was all black, but the rest looked to be in quite good shape.

"It's not much, I'm afraid," he said and handed it to Josie. She looked into the drawer. It was his Bible. It was a well-used Bible. The surrounding leather had its wear and tear. Inside it were several bookmarks. Mostly cards with a picture of Jesus or an angel and a Bible verse, and there was an embroidered cross. The other item in the drawer was an old lock. It was an old model, but it looked rather unused.

"This is perfect," she said as she looked at the Bible.

"And the lock. Do you want that as well?"

"Sure, these two items sum up Jack's life," she said and smiled. Chief Henderson had a confused look on his face, begging Josie to explain. "All his life, he worked at the hardware store, hence the lock. And all his life, he was faithfully going to the Salvation Army, with the Bible under his arm."

"Well, I'm glad we could help."

"You were very helpful. I think his cousin will appreciate this."

Josie took the lock out of the drawer and held it together with the Bible.

Chief Henderson returned to the other firefighters and gave them a thumbs-up, and soon the house was in full flames for the second time in a week. Only this time, the fire was a lot more controlled. Josie looked at the burning house. This tiny town had seen two fires, and each time, it had cost the life of a person. Josie walked on, leaving the crowd and the burning house behind her, heading for the lonely trail and hopefully some inspiration.

# Chapter 19

She had followed several trails and, as a consequence, walked in a huge circle around Kayne. Now she was back at her office and all she had gained on the walk was an enormous appetite. Apart from that, her thoughts had been all over the place. Would Carl be able to attend the funeral, would Frank and George be able to attend, and act civil toward each other? She thought she'd better pay them a visit and talk it over with them. She made a note. That would take even more off her sermon-preparing time. Still, the one thing lingering in her head most of all was Deirdre. She had hoped the trip to Seattle could provide her with some answers, but in reality, it had just given her more questions. Why had she dropped out of the training college and why had she not told anyone? She made herself some tomato soup and warmed some bread rolls she had picked up at the store on her way home. She was eating and had a legal pad where she planned to write notes about the speech. All she had written so far was: 'visit Frank.' Then she wrote: 'D - pregnant???'

Of course, there was no way she would find out about that now. But what could be the personal reason if it wasn't? She wasn't smoking. George had been absolutely certain of that. What else could count as a personal reason? Claire was right. If it was a legit reason that in some way wasn't considered shameful, then she surely would have given the reason. If she had just had a change of heart, she wouldn't cry while writing the letter. Still, there were traces of tears on the paper.

Josie finished the soup and went to her kitchen and put the plate in water. She thought about how weird it was. She was planning the funeral of Jack and all she could think about was someone who died more than forty years ago. Both deaths seemed equally dramatic. Of course, Deirdre was much younger than Jack, something which made it more tragic. Jack's death was tragic enough for the police to start a routine investigation.

Josie stopped her train of thought. What if they did routine investigations like this in the seventies as well? Then they would have something on Deirdre.

But how could she get her eyes on reports from the investigations? This was where the private investigator in books used to call in a favor of someone in the precinct. She didn't have any favors to call in. In fact, she hardly knew anyone. Her only option was Fred, and he was a bit intrigued by her 'investigation.' She googled the number and called before she regretted it. She had to call in at the reception.

"Spokane Sheriff department," a nice female voice answered at the other end.

"Could I speak to Inspector Fred Becker, please?"

"And who can I tell him is calling?"

"Josie Facundo, from Kayne," she answered. She wouldn't draw the Army into her investigation, so she left out her job title.

"And the reason for your call is?" The voice at the other end was still nice and not at all suspicious. Josie guessed it was all routine questions. She would have liked it better, though, if Fred had given her a card with his direct number. They always did that in the TV shows.

"He was up here in Kayne doing a routine investigation of a fire. It's about that." She hoped that would be sufficient for her to be transferred to Fred. The real reason for her call was not something she wanted to be broadcasted over the entire station.

"Just a minute," she said and Josie heard waiting music on the line.

"Hello, Josie," Fred answered less than a minute later. His response was forthcoming, almost eager, and it made Josie hesitate slightly. She had been pretty certain that he, despite what everyone else in Kayne seemed to think, had no other than the friendly intention of inviting her to lunch. Now, in the way he answered, she feared she could be wrong. It could also be that he was afraid she would consider him cheesy to invite her out, and now was relieved that she had contacted him.

"Hello, it's me."

"I know, that's why I said Josie," he answered. "What can I do for you?"

"This is just a giant waste of your time," she said a bit tentatively. "but I wondered if you could help me in my trivial investigation up here in Kayne."

"Sure, we detectives must stick together." She could hear the sarcasm in his voice, but it was not hostile.

## LIKE SMOKE IN THE WIND

"You said you always made a routine investigation when someone died in a fire. Does that mean there was an investigation when Deirdre Chisholm died as well?"

"I would guess so."

She told him about her trip to Seattle and what she had learned and what they suspected.

"So you need me to check if there's anything about a pregnancy?"

"Yes."

"If they did an autopsy, they would know, but I'm not sure they would do that." He sounded a bit reserved. "It's a long shot, but it's an intriguing long shot. I'll see what I can do."

"Thank you, Fred, you're the best."

"It may take some time, so if you'll give me your number, I'll call you when I've pulled the file."

She gave him her number, and they hung up.

*Now I can't keep on procrastinating any longer*, she thought. Then she looked at the list of scripture passages she made in the morning. They were all from the Bible. They all were a part of the word of God. It shouldn't make any difference whatever passage she chose. She took the first one: Psalms, number five. *I'll use this no matter what.* She read the passage several times and started taking notes down on her legal pad. For once, actual notes, the kind that would bring her closer to completing her sermon.

After about an hour, her phone rang, showing a number she hadn't seen before.

"Hello, this is Josie at the Salvation Army in Kayne," she answered. She guessed it was Fred, but couldn't be entirely certain.

"It's Fred here. Now I've got the file from the Deirdre case in front of me. And..." Fred waited as if to give time for a drum roll. "She was pregnant, about five to six weeks on."

"That explains why she withdrew from the college, but..." She hesitated. "...it brings on some new questions."

"Like who's the father?" Fred broke in.

"Sure, like that. I guess it says nothing about that."

"No, all it says about the pregnancy is that they chose not to tell her father."

"So George doesn't know. Isn't that mean?"

"Remember, this was the seventies and you're in a conservative part of the nation. Having a child out of wedlock wasn't considered a good thing. I guess they thought they did both Deirdre and George a favor."

"Really?"

"Sure, I've heard of families that cut off all contact with daughters that got pregnant, and still don't talk to them."

"Okay." Josie shook her head. She couldn't think of a single thing she could do that would make her mother stop talking to her. The worst part was that so much of this was done in the name of the Lord. And she knew Jesus didn't turn away from sinners. He turned toward them. "Does it say anything more?"

"The reason was probably a glow from a cigarette. They found cigarette butts inside."

"That doesn't make any sense. She didn't smoke. Could the butts have been there from earlier?"

"They couldn't have been too old. But that isn't the most interesting part."

"What is?"

"Guess who found her?"

"I don't know."

"Jack Sutton; he found her right after the fire in the mill had started, but the old lock had, by accident, jammed and locked the door. He struggled for twenty minutes to get her out, and when she finally got out, she had inhaled so much smoke that she was already dying."

"Was Jack the father?"

"Could be. They would have been around the same age."

"Well, thank you so much," Josie said.

"No problem. By the way, if you're ever in Spokane, look me up and I'll find a place where the burgers are edible."

"I will, and thank you again."

They hung up and Josie registered his phone number, just in case. She found a fresh page in her legal pad and wrote a D in the center and drew a circle around it. From there, she drew lines to other bubbles around it. One with Jack and a question mark. One stated 'Did George know.' Another one with 'not alone' and a last one with 'smoking in the mill.'

She looked at the page; Deirdre sure had secrets, but what secret did Jack refer to? And was it the same thing that made George and Frank become

## LIKE SMOKE IN THE WIND

enemies at the same time as she died? Jack was probably the only one she could flat out just ask about it, but now he was dead. The rest she felt like she had to lure the truth out of, by pretending she was talking about something entirely different.

# Chapter 20

"Nice of you to visit an old man. Please do come in." Frank stood in the door of the tiny cabin. His cabin lay on the outskirts of Kayne. Old people in the town would argue that all the houses this high up were outside Kayne. Frank's cabin lay among the highest houses, and even around a three hundred yards to go after she had passed the last house. But the view was impeccable. The entire valley, surrounded by snow-capped mountains, and with the setting sun painting a red and golden glow on the sky, not much in the world could compete with the view up here. Frank moved aside to let Josie in.

"Thanks for having me," she replied upon entering. She entered straight into the living room of the cabin. And what looked like a cabin on the outside looked even more so on the inside. The fireplace was made of natural stone and the ceiling had large exposed beams.

"It's cozy here," she added.

"It's small, but plenty for me. Please sit down," he said and pointed to some chairs before he went over to the kitchen. It was two similar chairs, but one seemed to be far more worn than the other. Josie assumed that was his regular chair, and seated herself in the other one.

"I used to live over the store, but when my wife died and Jonathan took over the store, it made more sense that he moved in there, so I ended up here," he shouted from the kitchen.

"Sure," Josie replied.

"It's tea, isn't it?" His head looked out from the kitchen.

"Yes." She nodded as she answered.

A moment later, he came out balancing a tray with a tea pot, two cups, and a plate with some cake on it.

"I can't bake, so the cake is from Bernie's."

"That's what you will get if you visit me too," Josie said and smiled. Josie felt an air of relief when Frank managed to put the tray down on the table without breaking anything. He started immediately pouring tea into both cups.

## LIKE SMOKE IN THE WIND

"I usually drink coffee, but it's not good to drink too much, so I thought I'd just join you on the tea," he said and smiled. The chair creaked as he sat down. "What do you use in the tea?"

"Nothing."

"Not milk, but surely some sugar?" Frank was halfway to putting a spoon full of sugar into Josie's cup. Josie quickly put her hand over the cup to prevent the coming disaster.

"No sugar and no milk."

"But, surely..." Frank objected. Josie held her hand over her cup as if she needed to physically stop Frank from pouring sugar in it, and finally, he drew the spoon back. "Well, I'll need a bit of sugar in my tea." He put three topped spoons with sugar into his tea.

Josie wasn't sure there would be much of a health effect changing from coffee to tea when you added that much sugar.

"But cake? You'll eat cake?"

"Sure," she said. It was a typical grocery store chocolate cake of the kind you heat in the microwave oven for a minute. Josie took a piece of lukewarm cake and placed on her plate.

"I am preparing for Jack's funeral. Normally, I would talk to the family to get some notes for the obituary, but he didn't have much family, and I guess you were all part of his family." Josie pulled a pen and notebook out of her bag.

"I would have to agree with you there. He worked in my shop for over fifty years."

"That's a long time. He must have been quite young when you hired him?"

"Sure, only a boy. You see, I felt bad for Grandma Sutton, that old lady bringing up two kids on her own. So I hired them to help her out."

"Them?"

"Yes, Jack and Carl. You couldn't find two kids more opposite. Jack was hardworking and trustworthy as the day was long, while Carl..." Frank shook his head. "I had to let him go."

"But Jack worked with you his whole life?" She had heard of Frank's dislike of Carl, so she tried to keep the focus on Jack.

"Sure." Frank took a long sip of his tea and made a slight wrinkle of his nose and put another teaspoon of sugar in his cup. "Sure you don't want any?" he said and held up the sugar cup.

89

"Yes, I'm good," Josie said, and cringed at the thought of all the sugar in Frank's cup.

"Only job he ever had, and only one he ever needed," Frank said with an air of pride.

"How was he as a person? I never really got to know him because of this disease he had."

"You can take your notebook up and down this town, but won't find anyone who can say a bad word about Jack. He was quiet and hardworking."

Josie smiled, talking to the employer. Good work ethics was probably the best praise he would get. She was glad she had others who had given a different account of Jack. She dreaded the thought of standing at the funeral, and all she could say was that he was a hard worker and an early riser. She picked up the cake and took a tiny, almost unnoticeable bite of it.

"It was sad with this dementia, so young; he should've had so many more years."

This was the first sign of real mourning she saw in Frank. He was right, she thought. Frank must be around twenty years older and was clear as the day. He didn't walk as fast anymore, but apart from that, he was in a remarkably good shape. And so many of his generation were in the same good health. It had been one of the first things she had noticed when she moved to Kayne a little over a year ago: how many old people lived here. That was, of course, due to so many younger ones moving out to more central areas. Then she had noticed how good shape all the old people were in. Her first thought was that walking up and down these hills all their lives had given them good health. Later, she had also realized that living in Kayne with poor health was impossible, so the old people with poor health ended up in Ashville. Jack, of course, had excellent health for his age, but his memory was his problem. So even if he was much younger than Frank, he couldn't take care of himself.

"Yes, it was really sad."

"Well, that's life," he mumbled.

The conversation went into a pause. They just sat there without talking and took a sip of the tea while she mustered strength for the hard part of the conversation. The tea had cooled just enough for her to take a long sip. She felt warm tea down her throat before she inhaled and slowly exhaled.

"I must ask one favor of you," she said.

## LIKE SMOKE IN THE WIND

"Sure, just name it."

"I know Carl isn't your favorite person in this town. But he is Jack's cousin and nearest kin. I need you to behave decently to him during the funeral."

"Of course I will. You didn't need to ask. That goes without saying. What would Carl do without Jack? He always looked after Carl."

"Good," she said and nodded. She had thought the same thoughts, or at least similar thoughts. Jack was the primary reason people in Kayne tolerated Carl. Without Jack, she feared life in Kayne could take a turn for the worse for poor Carl.

"And there's another thing as well."

"Okay, fire away." Frank smiled like nothing could change his good mood.

"I know you and George have your differences, but you are both going to be at the funeral, and I need you both to behave."

The good mood didn't last.

"I guess that is something you should ask him. Or even better, you should ask him not to come."

"You know he must be allowed to come as well."

"Why should he? You know what?"

"No." Josie tried to be the calm opposite of Frank, who by now was bright red in his face.

"I think George was the one who set Jack's house on fire."

He sat on the edge of his chair and pointed at Josie, as if she was a part of it. His breathing was faster and Josie feared he would come down with a heart attack or something.

"How can you even think that?" Josie forgot all about being calm, and almost shouted at Frank.

"He's done it before, you know," Frank said low, almost in a whisper. The roles were reversed and Frank was the one keeping his calm. "He set fire to that old mill, with his daughter inside."

"Deirdre?" Josie realized that this was the totally improper response to his allegations, but it was the first time someone besides Jack had mentioned Deirdre without her first squeezing it out of them.

"Sure, I don't know if he knew she was inside the mill when he torched it, or if that was deliberate. But he torched the mill and thus caused the death of Deirdre."

For a brief second, Josie thought maybe George had heard of the pregnancy after all. She thought of Fred's words of how embarrassing and humiliating having a child out of wedlock had been in these parts. George was surely a person who was preoccupied by his honor. Could it be that he killed her just to avoid the scandal? It took her only a second to regain her composure and realize just how crazy these allegations were.

"Frank, you cannot throw around accusations like that. It's crazy." Josie was no longer the one of them being calm and collected. She knew George blamed Frank for the death of Deirdre, but she had no idea it was the other way around as well.

"Is it? But I've got proof."

"Proof? What proof?" she asked.

"Among the old papers that I have stored, I have a paper that proves it."

"A paper that proves that George killed his own daughter?" Josie looked at Frank with disbelief in her eyes. She was pretty sure that hardware stores rarely had written murder-confessions in their archives.

"Maybe not that he actually killed her, but I have proof that all he is saying about this is a lie." Frank was uneasy in his seat with Josie's eyes almost drilling a hole through him.

"If you don't have proof that he killed her, then you don't say it, okay?" Josie had regained her calm, but her voice still trembled with anger. "If you have proof of any wrongdoing, then you should provide it to the proper authorities, or else keep your mouth shut."

"Maybe I will do that," he said and nodded.

"I need you to act like an adult at the funeral. For Jack's sake; he would have none of this."

"I know." Frank looked down, and Josie could see the memory of Jack had replaced the focus in his mind from that silly argument he had going with George. "Jack deserves better."

"He does," Josie said. For the next minutes, they sat in silence, only interrupted by the ticking from a clock. It had to be one of those modern cheap clocks with a plastic-sounding ticking. Josie guessed it was in the kitchen somewhere. She had thought that finding the reason for Frank and George's quarrel and pointing out how silly it was would be sufficient to end this great schism that had divided this city for half a century now. But realizing that they

# LIKE SMOKE IN THE WIND

actually both accused each other of murder was certainly not a tiny, trivial thing as she first supposed. Assuming they both believed it as well, it was not an easy solve. Anyhow, Josie was determined that it was probably more important than ever that someone got to the bottom of this. They needed to be convinced that it was an actual accident before they could lay it behind them. But how could she prove it was an accident? It happened forty years ago, and no one would talk about it. Of course, she didn't know that it was an accident either.

"You don't eat much cake," Frank said, and interrupted her train of thoughts.

"The problem is that I do eat a lot of cake," Josie countered. "I get served cake almost everywhere I go. And I have to taste the cakes everywhere as well. So my solution is to just eat tiny portions each time."

Frank nodded. "When I think of the officers before you, I believe it is an old problem in this town."

"I fear it's a problem officers face everywhere. I hope I haven't offended you," she said, and gave him an apologetic smile.

"No, no, I'm not offended at all. Maybe Sharon at the grocery store is," he said and laughed.

"Well, let's not tell her. By the way, you remembered that I drink tea," she said and lifted her cup in the air before she took a sip. "And for that, I am grateful."

"Of course I do. Do you want some more?"

"No, I'd better be on my way soon." She emptied the rest of the cup in one big sip.

"Well then, thanks for stopping by and I hope I could be of some help."

"You sure were, thank you. Can I read a verse from the Bible and say a prayer before I leave?"

"Sure," he said and nodded slowly as to confirm that he knew it was the price to have the officer visiting.

# Chapter 21

There was a flowery scent in the Army hall. They had stacked chairs closer together to make room for a wider mid-aisle and more chairs than they usually needed. The Army flag had a white bandoleer, and in front of the platform at the center of the hall stood Jack's casket. It was covered in flowers; the platform was covered in flowers. It had started early this morning, coming from several floral shops in Ashville.

Carl sat in the first row, looking sharp in the thrift store suit that Josie had bought him. He was sober and clean-shaven and looked quite good. It had come at a price. They had gone through his cabin and removed all the liquor they could find. They had made sure he never was alone over any longer stretch. Jonathan and Jerry had helped Josie with keeping him company. He had done nothing but swear and curse at them for days, but this morning when he was clean and sober in his new suit, Josie helped him with his tie, and he had uttered a slight thanks. Carl was the only family present at the funeral, but that didn't stop the funeral from being packed. Everyone knew and cared for Jack. And now, everyone came to pay their respects. The pianist played a classical piece that Josie didn't know, but she could tell it was in a minor key. Josie sat on the platform and looked at her hands. They were trembling, and she could not hold them still. It was her first funeral ever as an officer in the Salvation Army and she felt like a nervous wreck. She had hoped that her first few funerals would be old people and natural causes. The ones where people said that it was his time now and things like that. Jack was an old man, but many in the hall today were way older, and it certainly wasn't a natural cause. His Bible was one of the few things that was saved from the fire, and now it lay in front of her, because this was the one she was using for the sermon.

The funeral had started ten minutes late because of all the people that needed to find a place. The eulogy had gone well, and the representative from the undertaker, a young man in a black suit, had read the flower messages on all the flowers. Ms. Jensen played out the last tone of the hymn before the sermon

# LIKE SMOKE IN THE WIND

and Josie clutched Jack's Bible and got up on her shaky feet and moved for the pulpit.

"For the sermon today, I will read Psalm number five," she said. She had used one of Jack's bookmarks so she could flip it open on the right spot.

"I will read the whole psalm," she said and cleared her voice. "Listen to my words, Lord,

consider my lament.
Hear my cry for help,
my King and my God,
for to you I pray.
In the morning, Lord, you hear my voice;
in the morning I lay my requests before you
and wait expectantly."

Several in the rows nodded as she read, but no one ever commented during a sermon like you could hear in churches down south. A slight nod was as charismatic as they got.

"For you are not a God who is pleased with wickedness;
with you, evil people are not welcome.
The arrogant cannot stand in your presence."
You hate all who do wrong;
you destroy those who tell lies."

George peeked over to where Frank sat. They both went regularly to the Army, but somehow they had found a schedule so they didn't have to meet. But sometimes, like during funerals, they needed to both attend. George looked over at his sworn enemy and hoped the words about the wicked wrongdoers sank into his heart.

"The bloodthirsty and deceitful
you, Lord, detest.
But I, by your great love,
can come into your house;
in reverence I bow down
toward your holy temple."
Lead me, Lord, in your righteousness
because of my enemies—
make your way straight before me.

95

Not a word from their mouth can be trusted;
their heart is filled with malice."

Frank met George's eyes for a brief second. With the words of the deceitful, his eyes had automatically been drawn to George. When he noticed George looked back at him, he immediately looked away. Josie stopped shortly and swallowed before she continued.

"Their throat is an open grave;
with their tongues they tell lies.
Declare them guilty, O God!
Let their intrigues be their downfall.
Banish them for their many sins,
for they have rebelled against you.
But let all who take refuge in you be glad;
let them ever sing for joy."

Josie paused her reading. She had been speed-reading from verse two to verse eleven. Whenever holding a sermon, she preferred reading a longer passage of scripture rather than single verses and fragments of the text. The problem with the psalms was that even though they contained many nice passages, they would almost always contain a few verses of malice and revenge. It was a part of the psalm, so she had read it, but she read it considerably faster than she would read the last part of the psalm. Now she took a deep breath of air and could feel her heart rate going back to normal.

"Spread your protection over them,
that those who love your name may rejoice in you.
Surely, Lord, you bless the righteous;
you surround them with your favor as with a shield."

She laid down the Bible and picked up her neatly written notes. She had printed out the finished manuscript at 2 a.m., before she went to bed, and had read them several times after she got up this morning. Most likely she knew the sermon by heart, but there was no way she was going to leave her notes behind.

"It's a psalm of David, and it's a psalm about life. This psalm surely reflects the life of King David as we know it. Most of his life, he was at war. Enemies surrounded him. Even though our lives are not comparable to the life of David. Luckily, there is no army standing outside Kayne waiting to invade."

# LIKE SMOKE IN THE WIND

She spotted a few smiles and even some chuckles in the aisles. This was a funny thing she had experienced. If you are telling people a joke, they expect something funny, and if it isn't funny enough, they won't laugh. But in a sermon, nobody expects anything but seriousness. Then, if you tell them something that is not so serious, they will smile and even laugh at something that really isn't funny at all, only because it relieves the tension of the sermon. This had unfortunately led some preachers to believe that they were genuinely funny, and they started telling jokes, but they only received the occasional polite laugh. Josie noted the same was true for funeral sermons as well.

"Still, our lives, just like David's, will have their ups and downs. We all have our good days, we all have our hard spells. That's life. And that's how life was for Jack as well. And maybe it is fair to say that Jack's life had more rough passages than easy ones."

More people nodded, and Carl wiped a tear from his right eye.

"But what can we learn from the Psalm of David, and how can Jack's example inspire us?" Josie paused to let the question sink in. "Surely there's a longer passage where David rants over his enemies and prays the Lord to end them. I believe that David prayed to the Lord to harm his enemies, and..." she said and hesitated slightly. "I am absolutely sure that God refused to listen. But I also believe he listened again toward the end of the psalm. Let all who take refuge in you be glad. The past week, I have been talking to many of you about Jack, and it has been a delight to hear all the good things you have to say about him. He, just like David, wasn't a perfect man. He also had his share of hardship and struggles. But he was one of those who sought refuge in the Lord. That gave him hope and comfort in his life, and it gives us hope and comfort today. Because the Lord who granted him refuge when he, as a boy, lost both his parents in that tragic accident. And who granted him refuge when he, as a young man, lost Grandma Sutton, and he and Carl were all alone."

Talking about the hardship Jack had faced, she could mention the loss of Deirdre as well. They were clearly close, and it was a great blow to him. But really, how close? Did he lose a child as well on that same night as Deirdre died? Was that the secret that he kept all the way to his grave? Of course, she couldn't disclose any of this. It would have led to an uproar. So she stuck with the loss of his parents and Grandma Sutton. "The same Lord is still keeping him in his refuge. So back to my initial question: what can we learn from King David's and

# ISAAC LIND

Jack's example? For the first, and mind you, now I'm probably thinking more of David than of Jack. You can seek refuge in the Lord, no matter how imperfect you are. God doesn't sort out the best candidates, no he meets everyone with open arms. And Jack did just that." Josie told them about his faithfulness at the Salvation Army according to the testimonies people had given on his behalf. She suspected that in his young days, his motivation had been a bit like the rest of the boys in Kayne. The girls went to the Army, so the boys went along. Still, he had continued after the girls were married or had moved away. "Jack chose the Lord early in life and stuck with it. And maybe Jack saw something clearer than the rest of us. We all have our family to support us, and maybe that can make it harder to realize that we need the Lord. But Jack was all alone and maybe that helped him to see." She had been in doubt if she should have this as a part of the sermon. After all, the main person at this funeral, and the only living relative, Carl, was even more of a loner than Jack. But even though Carl wasn't frequenting the Army meetings, every time she had been up to his cabin with food when he had a rough spell in his life, he always appreciated that she read from his Bible. Now she could see Carl slowly nodding his head. His life was so different from everyone else present, but the same Lord had granted him refuge as well.

"Both King David and Jack sought the refuge in the Lord, and I believed they both found a place where they were safe, and where they weren't alone. The most important thing we can learn from Jack's example is to seek refuge in the lord. Amen" She put the notes in the Bible and closed the book. Her hands were no longer trembling, but her shirt was soaking wet and she was so glad she had a jacket on to cover it up. Slowly, she walked down from the platform and stood in front of the casket.

The six men assigned to carry the casket were all in black suits, most of them in a design that was popular some time in the nineties. Josie stretched out her hand toward Carl. Normally, the minister would go before the casket and the family after, but here the family was one person, and he shouldn't be alone. Carl got up and took her hand and clutched it. Hard. Like it was the only thing holding him in this world. It felt like the blood circulation in her hand had stopped. Josie smiled at him. The piano played, and together they marched slowly out of the hall. The casket and soon the entire congregation followed close by.

# Chapter 22

Kayne had no cemetery of its own, so they placed the casket in the funeral car. Then everyone followed, in a long line of cars, the ten miles to the cemetery outside Ashville. It was a slow procession, taking almost a half an hour to get there, and less than ten minutes to get back. Josie was so focused on the job that she was almost in a haze of nerves and anxiety until she had performed all her duties. It was with a sigh of relief she concluded with the last word of the last hymn.

Then followed a strange scene that, at least on the periphery level, was a beautiful thing. As the only relative attending, Carl stood there and received the condolences from the entire town. People that never spoke to him, or that wouldn't even look him in the eyes. People who had tolerated him merely as a favor to Jack now shook his hand. This had to be a rare moment of inclusion in the Kayne society for Carl. Josie, however, was skeptical as to how long it would last. They had accepted him because of Jack; would they keep accepting him because of Jack, or would he soon become more of an outcast than what he ever had been? Josie feared the latter. But right now, Carl felt the heart-warming care from everyone attending the funeral.

Josie had drawn away from the crowd. She was giving Carl a lift, so she didn't need to line up to give her condolences. But she kept close enough to hear what was being said, out of pure curiosity. Frank and Jonathan were coming up to Carl, with George following not far behind. Josie had to admit that it impressed her with how those two had handled themselves at this funeral. She thought she ought to mention it to them sometime.

"I'm so sorry for your loss. He was a man of honor," Frank said and shook Carl's hand. Carl nodded and said something Josie couldn't quite hear, but probably just a plain 'thank you.' This had to be one of the harder handshakes for Carl, given their history.

"What did you say?" Frank shouted. Josie's first concern was that Carl's response had been something entirely different from the simple 'thank you' she expected. Then she realized Frank had turned and was looking at George.

"You heard me. I called you a liar," George shouted back.

"You take that back," Frank said and moved toward George. For a moment, Josie feared the old men were actually starting a fight at their friend's funeral.

"You don't have the emotional capacity to feel sorry when someone dies, and that's the truth."

"What you mean by that?"

"You know exactly what I mean."

By this time, Jonathan and Jerry had caught up with their fathers and the potential fight was called off. At least for the time being.

"For years, you have tried to pin your daughter's death on me." Frank was red in his face as he stood there, pointing at George. Jonathan held him back so he could not reach him. "But it was your inadequacy as a parent that killed her, and back home, I have a paper that proves it."

Josie guessed it was the same piece of paper he had mentioned to her yesterday. She could see how jaws were dropping all around the crowd. Not that they hadn't feared this, but no one really expected them to break out in a full-fledged fight during Jack's funeral.

"You're just a filthy liar," George shouted back while Jerry was pulling him away. Jonathan and Jerry pulled each of their fathers back to their car. It took some minutes before the rest of the crowd got back to normal. Josie thought she at least didn't have to worry about them at the reception afterwards.

"Just give me five minutes and I'll make us some tea," she had said before she disappeared up into her apartment. Ernie had waited for her down in the office. They would go through the books and update them after the funeral. "Let's do it while it's fresh. It is so easy to forget later on," Ernie had said. Josie used the time efficiently. Time to boil hot water and three minutes for the tea to brew. That gave her just enough time to get out the uniform, take a wet cloth and wash off the worst and slip into something more comfortable. She came down

## LIKE SMOKE IN THE WIND

the stairs with a tray containing tea and some crackers, wearing sweatpants and a large t-shirt.

"Sorry, but I was drenched in sweat," she said as she entered the office.

"I understand. It's normal to be nervous." Ernie smiled, probably eager to get out of his uniform as well. "But you did really well today. No one ever noticed that this was your first."

"Thanks."

"By the way, it's not the first funerals I fear. It's the last."

"What you mean by that?" Josie asked.

"Some years ago, when Mrs. Olson's husband passed away, Mrs. Olson asked an old retired major to hold the funeral. The old major had been at Kayne many years ago, and he had meant a lot to the Olsons back then. It was a good thought. The only problem was that he was getting forgetful in his old days, so during the funeral, he called Robert Olson Bob Jensen, John Swanson, and Ben Jensen. Not once did he call the deceased by his right name. It was a nightmare," Ernie said and laughed so hard, his entire body was shaking.

"I hope someone will stop me before I reach that point."

"I guess you've got quite a few years before that's an issue." Ernie wiped tears out of his eyes.

"What books do we need?" Josie asked.

"There is a register for funerals, and we need the soldiers' roll."

Josie got up and searched through the file cabinet where the books were kept.

"Here's the soldiers' roll," she said and handed it to Ernie. "And this must be the register you talked about." She pulled up a red hardcover book the size of a legal pad.

"Yes, that's the one. Let's start with that." They filled out Jack's name, date of birth, date of death, and finally, the date of the funeral. Last, it was the name of the officer that had conducted the funeral. They both put their initials on the end of the line. Then Ernie found the soldiers' roll and started going through it before he handed it to Josie.

"I struggle to read that old handwriting. It's better you do it."

"Sure," Josie said and opened the book.

"It's in the adherent section."

Josie flipped to the back of the book and searched down the pages with her index finger.

"Hm, I guess I struggle a bit with some handwriting as well," she said as she tried to decode the names on each line.

"If someone as young as you struggles, you see why it's impossible for me." Ernie chuckled and took a sip of the tea Josie had brought him.

"So Carl is an adherent as well?"

"Sure, there's not many people in Kayne whose name you won't find in one of our books."

Josie nodded and continued to scroll down the pages.

"And look, Jerry's name is Gerald. I thought it was Jeremy," she said and smiled.

"Let me see," Ernie broke in. Josie flipped through the book and pointed. Ernie stretched his neck and straightened his glasses. "So it seems, I didn't know that, and I've gone through these books so many times."

Josie turned the book back and continued the search back in time.

"Here it is, Jack Sutton, enrolled May in seventy-six, and written out – you've got a pen," she said and reached her hand toward Ernie. He placed a ball-point pen in her hand and wrote today's date. "Reason G," she mumbled.

"Promoted to glory," Ernie said as a reference to the G in reason, and nodded. "And of that, there is no doubt in my mind."

"Was that it?" Josie asked and looked up from the book.

"Yup, make sure you show these to the DC next time he's in town so he can sign it too."

Josie picked up the books and placed them back in the cabinet.

"I hope it's long before we need these books again," she said, and regretted it as soon as she said it. The soldiers' roll would be used for the more festive occasions, like enrolling new soldiers and adherents. The problem was that in a place like Kayne, with most of the population, and therefore also the majority of the members, being elderly, the most likely use for the soldiers' roll was when people died.

"At least for that purpose," Ernie shot in.

"Sure, that's what I meant," she said apologetically.

"Well, I guess there are not many candidates to be enrolled at the moment, I fear," Ernie said and sighed.

# Chapter 23

At the beginning, it was just in her dream. She had been exhausted after the funeral, gone early to bed and promised herself to lie in. But it was one of these nights when her head was filled with too much stuff and she had this restless sleep. The worst part was the dreams. She would dream about all kinds of weird stuff. She dreamt of the funeral, and suddenly, a carpenter came in and started hitting his hammer around everywhere, and she had to make him stuff. Then she was chased by a bear. She escaped into a closet, but the bear was banging on the closet.

That was, of course, when she woke up, breathing heavily and trying to calm down her heart, which was rushing away. She fumbled around for her phone to check the time. Not yet six o'clock; she could go back to sleep for a few hours still. She rolled over to the other side and sighed in relief. She could still get a couple of hours of sleep. Then the banging started again. This time, it was the door; probably it had been the door all the time. She got up. At this hour, it had to be something serious. The banging was on the door to her apartment, so it had to be someone who could lock themselves in. She opened the door and Marge stood there at the top of the stairs.

"I'm sorry to wake you up, but it's..." she said and stopped and couldn't quite say.

"No problem," Josie said. If she had been woken up at nine o'clock, she'd probably put a smile on her face and insist that she already was awake, but this early, there was no point in pretending.

"It's Frank," she said and pointed in a direction that Josie was sure wasn't to Frank's house. "The cabin burnt to the ground last night."

"What?" At first, it sounded like a macabre prank, but she knew Marge would never joke about something like that. "I'll come."

Josie hurried to the bathroom and got her clothes on, washed her face and put her hair into a knot, and decided that would have to do. She could hear sirens from a fire truck as they rushed down the stairs. Out on the street, the acrid smell of burnt wood tore into her nostrils and gave her a flashback to the fire at Jack's house. Josie's urge to make haste was restrained by her inclination to wait for Marge. After all, she had taken the time to give the news to her. They had not come far up Silver Lake Road before Marge was wheezing, and Josie had to slow down her pace.

"You don't have to wait for me," Marge said, short-breathed. "You just go on, and I'll come later."

"No, it's okay. We'll walk together." Josie was reminded of a retired major that once had spoken to them at the training college. The topic was caring in crisis. "It is not a race," she remembered him saying. The best care givers in crises were rarely the ones who came first, but often the ones who left last. His message was that people had the tendency to be quick to offer condolences and quick to be done with it, while the people who experience the crisis could feel the pain for years, and sometimes for the rest of their lives. The hard part for them was that after some time, they had no one to talk to because everyone thought it was time to move on. Even though it wasn't quite related, it was a reminder that her most important job with this fire wasn't at the fire-site, but in the days and even months to come. Josie slowed down to a more manageable pace for Marge. As they got closer to Frank's cabin, more people were walking the same way, to see for themselves what had happened. When they arrived, the firefighter was already spraying water on the remains of the cabin. It seemed a little late. Even though thick black smoke was coming up from the ruins, she couldn't see any flames. The cabin's remote location was probably the reason it was almost totally burnt out before someone had contacted the fire department.

"Hello, Lieutenant," Chief Henderson greeted her with a dampened smile.

"Chief Henderson," Josie answered without a smile or any additional remarks. The usual 'nice to see you' just wouldn't fly in the situation. "What's the status?" Josie asked after a while.

"The alarm went off far too late. There is nothing to salvage here. If the resident is inside, something we do fear, there is no hope for him. We'll have to cool it down to make sure the fire doesn't spread to the forest."

Josie nodded. She could see that the firefighters were spraying just as much water on the surrounding forest as they did on the cabin.

"When it's all secured, we will search through the site."

## LIKE SMOKE IN THE WIND

"Is there anything I can do?"

"Well, there's a son over there." Chief Henderson pointed at Jonathan standing a few steps closer to the fire than the rest of the crowd, holding Lissie, his wife.

"Sure," she said, and walked over to Jonathan and Lissie, and held them both.

"Why?" Jonathan kept asking. None of them had any answer. Even though they hadn't found any body yet, they knew he had to be in there. Where else would he be? If he wasn't at home, he was at the store or visiting Jonathan, and they all knew he wasn't. Another facet of the why was in the question everyone was asking around the site. A town that had not experienced a serious fire for over forty years now had two in a week. What were the odds of a coincidence like that? Unless, of course, it wasn't an accident, Josie thought and guessed she could not be the only one thinking about it. Then, on the other hand, who could do something like this?

"I should head home. The store opens soon," Jonathan said after a while in silence.

"The store is closed today, Jonathan," Josie answered, and she could see the same thing written all over his wife's face. "No one will come today, because no one expects it to be open."

"But..." Jonathan tried to object. This store probably had not been closed for a whole day since it first opened. It closed for a few hours during Jack's funeral, and had been so for every other funeral of someone who was reasonably close. Josie admired the work ethic, but this was stupid.

"You don't even need to put up a note on the door. Everyone knows."

"Jonathan, we could use a day where we didn't have to smile at customers," Lissie broke in.

Jonathan nodded. "I guess you're right."

"But you should go home anyway, though. I'll drop by later on and give you an update on what the firefighters find, okay?" Josie said.

Lissie agreed and gently pulled Jonathan on the sleeve of his jacket. Jonathan nodded slowly and hesitatingly followed his wife over to their car, which was parked about a hundred yards down the road. As they walked by the crowd, people tapped them on their shoulders. It was the Kayne equivalent to a warm hug and two kisses on each cheek.

105

## ISAAC LIND

Josie stood by herself after Jonathan and Lissie left, feeling hollow and empty inside. She knew Frank, and she liked him. She felt like crying, but also that she couldn't. The crowd that gathered around the fire site was all friends and neighbors going decades back. Everyone knew Frank better than Josie, and she felt like she was the person who was least entitled to cry. She had felt the same way when Jack died, but then she had busied herself and buried the emotions in work. Now there was nothing she could do that made sense.

As she stood there fighting the tears she felt she wasn't entitled to shed, a large black Ford with the Sheriff Department of Spokane shield on both sides slowly made its way through the crowd. She spotted Fred Becker behind the wheel. It looked like he sent her a smile, but she really couldn't tell. Fred went right over to Chief Henderson, while the others spread the crowd. They politely asked everyone to leave and promised that they would keep them updated. It wasn't done in large proclamation to the entire crowd, but they went quietly from group to group and explained the situation. Everyone nodded and headed back home. Josie, who stood on the far end of where the police officers had started, didn't wait until she was told, but slowly moved back home along with the others.

"Lieutenant!" She had almost passed the police car when she heard Becker call out for her. She turned around and could see him wave her over.

"Yes, Inspector," she answered as she met up with him.

"We have to investigate this, and I hoped you could help us out."

"Sure, just name it."

"Frank, that's his name, isn't it?"

"Yes, Frank Meadows."

"He has a son living in town?"

"Yes."

"Anyone else?"

"I believe he has two daughters, one in Seattle and one in Spokane. He constantly talked of his grandchildren there as well."

"I need to talk to Jonathan first, I guess, but I must wait until we have examined the fire site. I will need a body before I start a murder investigation."

"So it is murder?"

"Too early to tell, but two fires with a deadly outcome in little over a week apart is a rare coincidence. We really need to pick this one apart."

106

## LIKE SMOKE IN THE WIND

"I promised to drop by Jonathan and Lissie later on. Do you want to tag along, or would you prefer to go on your own?"

"No, it would be nice to go with someone who knows them at this stage, at least."

"At this stage?"

"As I said, this could eventually turn into a murder investigation."

"I really can't believe there's anyone in Kayne that could be capable of killing someone," Josie said, more in a way of thinking out loud. "It would make more sense that it's someone from the outside."

"Statistically speaking," Fred broke her off, "it's not an outsider. They don't have too many dealings with out-of-towners, and nobody passes through Kayne. If it's murder, the killer almost certainly is a local."

Josie realized that what Fred told her made sense, but she really couldn't fathom that anyone in Kayne could have done this.

"We are ready to search through the site." It was Chief Henderson that informed Becker. Becker nodded.

"Are you somehow familiar with the layout of the cabin?" Henderson asked, addressing Josie.

"A bit. I've been here a few times." She described the layout of the cabin as best she could. Henderson nodded and passed the information on to the others.

"We need to search the perimeters. Would you like to join in?" Becker asked.

"Sure." Josie nodded. She felt the urge to wait and see what the firefighters found, and doing something was better than just waiting around.

The three police officers divided the area between them. Fred searched in front of the house, while the two others were in the back. Josie walked together with Fred.

"What are you looking for?" Josie asked.

"Anything that doesn't belong here, like this," he said, and picked up a plastic bottle, looking at it.

"This looks like it has been lying here for years, so it's not very interesting." They searched thoroughly through the shrubbery on the other side of the road in front of the house.

"A possible arsonist would probably avoid being seen, and therefore, maybe also avoided using roads. So we need to see if anyone passed through here last night."

They searched some more before Henderson called for them. Becker made sure he knew where he was before he returned to the fire site. This way, he was sure he didn't miss anything when he came back to continue the search.

"What you got for me?" Becker said as he approached the firefighters.

"We got a dead body. We can tell it's male, but there is not much to go on to ID him. I guess an autopsy will have to pull the dental records to confirm it."

Fred nodded. "Anything else?"

"We found him where Josie said the bedrooms lie, and the position indicates that he was asleep or at least in bed." Henderson paused slightly. It was obvious that even for a merited firefighter as Henderson, people dying in fires was still emotional. "It also looks like the fire originated in the area where he was found."

"So if he was smoking on his bed, that could be the reason?" Fred asked.

"Sure, but we can't be certain before we have concluded our investigation."

"How long will that take?" Fred asked

"We will only need a couple of days, but every sample we have to send away for analysis will easily take a week, so could the autopsy, depending on the queue."

"Well, thanks so far; it's sufficient for us to at least make a start."

Fred went to the back of the burnt-down cabin and informed the other police officers about the findings. Josie could see he was pointing to the front of the cabin as well. She guessed he wanted them to continue the search in front of the house.

"I guess it's time to visit his son," Fred said as he got back.

"Okay," Josie said and followed him over to his car.

# Chapter 24

Josie drove down with Fred, and he parked outside the hardware store. There was a note in the door's window stating that it was closed for the day. Fred stepped out, Josie felt more like she climbed out of the tall car.

"Give me two seconds. I'll just..." Josie said and pointed at the grocery store.

"Sure, no problem."

Josie disappeared into the shop next door, and came out a minute later with a large bag of fresh bread rolls.

"I'm not sure they'll think about getting some food on a day like this." She smiled and held up the bag.

"I think it's marvelous how you care for the locals."

"Not really. I missed my own breakfast and I'm starving," she replied.

"I'm not buying that one; remember, I saw you up at Carl's cabin as well."

Josie didn't answer. She just rounded the corner to the side of the hardware store. From there, they had stairs taking them to Jonathan and Lissie's apartment. She gently knocked on the door and they waited. They waited until she could see Fred was getting impatient, then she knocked once more. Harder this time. Now Jonathan came and opened the door.

"I brought the inspector, if you don't mind."

"Sure, come on in," he replied before he stepped aside and let them in. The living room was in a bright color on the walls and a dark hardwood floor that suggested that it was redecorated not that many years ago. Josie always thought it was nice, but then again, everything was nice compared to her fifty-year-old orange and brown linoleum.

"So nice of you to come," Lissie said as they stepped into the living room. She came over and gave Josie a hug before she greeted Fred.

"Have you eaten anything?"

Lissie shook her head.

"You must eat. I brought some bread rolls. Come and let's fix something."

# ISAAC LIND

Josie went to the kitchen with Lissie a step behind her. Fred and Jonathan were left behind, both being a bit baffled.

"What plates shall we use?" Josie asked and pointed to the upper cabinets. If it had been Jonathan, she would just take some plates, because that was what he would have done too. But she suspected Lissie would have an idea of what would be the right china for this occasion.

"Take the blue ones over in that cabinet," she said, and pointed at a tall wooden cabinet beside the dining table. Lissie started making coffee and tea, while she pulled out everything in the fridge that could be useful. She placed it all on the bench: some juice, a couple of different cheeses, ham and some different kinds of jams. Then she cut the bread rolls in halves. As Lissie made something ready, Josie put it on the table.

It all took about ten minutes and the table was set for four people. Fred looked uncomfortable as he sat there beside Josie.

Josie folded her hands and bowed her head. Jonathan and Lissie did the same, and Fred still looked a bit lost.

"Dear Lord, bless our food, and above all, bless Jonathan and Lissie today, and in days to come. Amen," Josie said.

"Amen," Fred repeated. He had found his composure and bowed his head in prayer as well.

Josie and Jonathan each took a bread roll, while Lissie started serving coffee and tea. Fred just looked at them before he finally cleared his throat.

"Lissie and Jonathan Meadows," he said. Josie could tell he had his official business police officer voice. They looked at him and nodded.

"I am afraid that I must inform you that there has been a dead body found in the ruins of your father, Frank Meadows', house. Most likely, it is the body of Frank Meadows."

Jonathan nodded. He had known this all morning, but still tears sprang into his eyes.

"I know, I know," he said. Josie reached over the table and clutched his hand. He sat there a minute with tears rolling down his face. Lissie found some tissue and handed it to him before she wrapped her arms around him in a warm embrace. He wiped away his tears.

"Let's eat, please, Inspector," he said and handed Fred the basket of bread rolls. Fred took one, and cut a piece of brie and some red pepper. For a long

# LIKE SMOKE IN THE WIND

time, they just ate and nobody said anything. It was obvious that Jonathan and Lissie had missed their breakfast as well.

"Is there any connection between Jack and your father?"

"Sure there is. Jack worked at my father's store his whole life. We had to let him go when his dementia got too bad, but until then, he was here every day."

"We can't overlook the possibility that these are not accidents but are connected incidents."

Jonathan nodded.

"Could it be that there's a connection to the hardware store?"

"I really can't see how," Jonathan said.

"The problem is that we can't really see that anyone would be capable of killing either Jack or Frank," Lissie shot in.

"Well, sometimes you just don't know people as well as you think," Fred replied. "It's important to us that we get all the information we can."

Jonathan and Lissie nodded.

"When did you last see Frank?"

"Yesterday. He was at Jack's funeral and then he ate dinner together with us."

"He often does," Lissie said. Josie noticed she referred to her father-in-law in present tense, but she reckoned they had harder issues to deal with than past and present tense right now.

"Did your father have any enemies?"

"Well." Jonathan hesitated. "The old man was a stubborn fool, and there's some other stubborn fools as well in this town."

"Like who?"

"George Chisholm, for one. He blamed my father for the death of his daughter. She died in the fire at the mill."

"Deirdre, wasn't it?" Fred said.

"Yes, and my father had promised to change the lock, because the old one didn't work, so that the place could be closed down. She burnt in the mill because the old lock malfunctioned. My dad, in turn, accused him back, meaning that the death of Deirdre somehow was his own fault."

"It was really just sad. Those two used to be best friends," Lissie added.

111

## ISAAC LIND

"And this was still going on?" Fred said, rather perplexed. He recalled Josie had said this was over forty years ago. Even though it was just like Josie had told him, he struggled to grasp the idea of carrying a grudge for so long.

"Sure, they had a big falling out only yesterday." Jonathan told him about the big argument between Frank and George at the funeral the day before.

"Don't get me wrong, Dad was a good man. He was fair, he helped people all the time. People liked him, but he was also quite stubborn."

"I see. Is there any other?" Fred inquired.

"My dad and Carl Sutton never got along."

"And why was that?"

"My dad hired both Jack and Carl when they were quite young, as a favor to Grandma Sutton. The old woman was left with the responsibility of raising two young boys, and he wanted to help. Carl was quite young. He ran some errands for Dad, and Dad gave him some pocket money. But at some point, he became unstable and unreliable and Dad had to let him go."

"When was this?"

"Around the same time as the mill burnt down, I guess," Lissie said. "That was when he started dropping out of school, and after Grandma Sutton died, it all fell apart for him."

Fred paused as he refilled his cup with more coffee.

"And Jack, did he fall out with anyone?"

"No, Jack was a different kind than my father."

"A bit more rounded in his edges," Lissie added.

"No one really disliked Jack?"

"No, not as far as I can tell," Jonathan said. "Now, when does this officially become a murder investigation?"

"When the fire investigation can conclude on the reason, and they'll have to look into the Jack fire once again."

Fred finished his bread roll and excused himself. Josie reckoned the combination of the official police business and a meal with a stranger was hard to juggle. She felt bad about putting him in this situation, but had hoped they could stay long enough for her to get a full breakfast.

"I'll stop by later," she said and hugged them both before they both left.

112

# LIKE SMOKE IN THE WIND

"So, you think it's a double homicide?" Josie asked Fred as they got back on the street.

"I try not to think too much at this stage. I believe it is somehow related."

"How can it be related and not be a double homicide?"

"Can we borrow some space in the Army and set up a field office for the investigation?"

"Sure, you can use the second hall, but you need to clear out on Sunday before the evening sermon."

"Good, hop in and I'll tell you how it can be related." They both climbed into the Ford. "I heard of a house burning down in a small rural village somewhere in Idaho once. They got money back on their insurance, and not long after, they had a brand new house with new furniture and everything." Fred stopped the car outside the Salvation Army hall. "Then, of course, the neighbors were getting jealous. So another house burnt down, and the same thing happened. Then another one and another one. Of course, the police and the insurance company got suspicious, and they investigated it and found that they had set fire to their houses themselves."

"But when people commit insurance fraud, they don't burn down the house when they're still inside," Josie said and got out.

"Okay, it's a poor example, but my point is: things can be connected even if it's not the same person behind it."

"Even if no one is responsible?" she asked as she unlocked the main door and held it open to Fred. "We'll just set up some tables here. You can use the printer in my office if you need. I'll fix you a spare key." Josie pointed at some tables in a corner that were folded and stacked away.

"Perfect," he said as a comment to the space she offered them. "My point is, the first fire was most likely an accident, but it still sparked the other ones."

"So you say that Jack dying could be an accident, but still could have inspired the murder of Frank?"

"There usually is something that kicks off a chain of events. It could be the death of Jack, it could be something else. I believe that somehow there is a link."

Fred's phone rang. He answered it. After several hm's, he told the person at the other end that he had set them up in the Army and they should meet.

"Well, it's a murder case now. We got the cause of the fire; gasoline was used and someone set fire to it from the outside. And they found a jerry can that just recently was thrown away in the shrubbery above his cabin." Fred sounded almost excited that it was a murder investigation. "Of course it's a quite different approach than with Jack, where the fire started inside the house."

"But Jack's house was easy to get inside," Josie said. "He always lost his keys somewhere, so in the end, they just stuck the key in on the outside so it would always be there."

"I remember Carl also mentioned that," he said and shook his head.

"This is Kayne, not Spokane, remember?"

# Chapter 25

A quick glance up and down the main street made sure it was empty before the dark figure moved toward the Salvation Army hall. He pulled a key-chain with three brand new keys out of his pocket. Three keys copied from Marge's key-chain. The second key opened the main door with ease. The two remaining keys should be one for the office and one for Josie's apartment. Slowly, the figure moved up the stairs, stepping only on the sides of the stairs. Old stairs could be deceitfully noisy, especially if one treaded at the middle of the stairs. At the top of the stairs, one of the remaining keys slid into the lock and made a low metallic clicking sound as the door unlocked. He breathed slowly, listening for any sound that might indicate that Josie, despite the hours and darkness in the apartment, wasn't asleep.

No sound at all was detected. A glove-covered hand moved the door handle slowly, and the door was pushed in. The apartment had a tiny hallway with two doors besides the one into the apartment. Straight ahead, there was one door into the bathroom, the one with a heart on, and on the left, one door into the living room that had a semi-transparent window in. From the living room, there was a door leading to the kitchen at one end, and two bedrooms on the other end. The living room was divided in two, one part with the sofa, a coffee table and a TV set. The other part with a bookshelf and a dining table. It was clear that she used the dining table for some work. A legal pad still rested on the table. The dark figure moved over to the table and flipped through the legal pad. It was notes for sermons and to-do lists. He stopped flipping on a page containing a brainstorm page with a D at the center.

"This, Josie, is why I'm here. Because you can't keep your nose out of other people's business," the person whispered to himself.

He closed the legal pad and moved over toward the bedroom doors. The first door served as a guest room or maybe a storage, considering all the mess. It was closed carefully and the next door was slowly opened. The room was chilly and dark. It was the master bedroom and had a queen-size bed. Josie lay in the middle of it. He moved over to the end of the bed and looked at Josie. She lay absolutely still. The person pulled a knife up from the pocket; the blade was released with a little snap and he held it up in the air. Killing her like this, and no one would think it was an accident. But maybe it could be arranged as a suicide?

*Well, if it should come to this, it probably doesn't matter,* he thought. For now, she could live, but it was reassuring to know that the keys worked and this could be done if she should get any closer to figuring out the truth of Deirdre Chisholm. He folded the knife and put it back into his pocket, and moved slowly out of the bedroom. The door was carefully closed, and he moved toward the little hallway. As the living room door was closed, the door of the bedroom opened and Josie came out. The person moved quickly away from the window in the door and pulled the knife once more. The dark silhouette of Josie standing in the middle of the living room floor and looking around was visible through the window in the living room door.

She stood there a brief moment before she moved over to the kitchen and found herself a glass and turned on the tap and waited for the water to get cold.

The person in the hallway used the chance to sneak out and lock the door when the tap ran. He moved down the stairs in the same way as coming up, and a minute later, the person was out on the street and away from the Salvation Army.

Josie stood in her kitchen with her glass of water. Another of the perks of living here. She could drink water straight out of the tap. Putting down the glass, she wiped her mouth with the back of her hand. She stopped once more as she got back into the living room. There was something strange about it. She had woken up with the strange feeling of having someone in her room. And now she stood there and couldn't quite put her finger on it. Was there an unfamiliar smell? She couldn't quite tell. Sometimes, living in an old house freaked her out. Especially when the wind was blowing, it made so many strange sounds. And, of course, there could be some strange smells in a house of this age? Josie shook her head.

## LIKE SMOKE IN THE WIND

"Don't get paranoid now, Josie," she said to herself before she got back into her room and crawled into bed. Only a few minutes later, she was fast asleep.

# Chapter 26

Josie slowly passed the shelves in the grocery store in search of something to make for dinner. She originally came down because she lacked bread for breakfast, but did all the shopping she needed at the same time. Bread, butter and eggs and so on were easy to check off the list, but dinner was the tricky one. Then she had to figure out what to make first, and that was the eternal hassle. When she first came to Kayne, she missed the large malls you'd have in even small cities. She missed shopping for her food in a huge Walmart or a Kroger. The local grocery store was only a fraction of a regular Walmart. It was like they had nothing here. After a while, she realized that the main difference was not in what they offered, but how many sorts of everything they offered. Here, they had one brand of pasta and five variations, instead of twenty brands with ten variations of each. What she couldn't get were special sauces and rare spices. But those things often had long expiration dates, so she could bulk up every time she was out of town. The only issue she was left with was that they didn't carry her favorite chocolate. This one she couldn't bulk buy because then she would overeat for a few days and be out of chocolate anyway. It had resulted in her eating less chocolate, and that was okay because she ate more cake up here.

So, in time, she had grown fond of the grocery store, or Bernie's, as the locals called it. It never felt natural for Josie to call it Bernie's because she never knew Bernie. Frank's for the hardware store was different because she knew Frank. The grocery store had most of the things she needed, and shopping usually went faster when the selection was smaller. Unless when she wasn't sure of what she wanted. Except right now. With all the pressures of funerals and all the rumors going on around Kayne the past few weeks, she had absolutely lost her appetite. She had eaten far too often at the diner. Now she had decided to cook herself a proper meal, but she had no idea what. She looked at a bag of pasta, then shook her head, then she picked up some rice and put it back down. Finally, her eyes rested on the vegetable stand. The vegetables looked great this

# LIKE SMOKE IN THE WIND

time of year, and she remembered how bleak and gray the stand had become during winter. That settled it, something with vegetables.

Josie was heading for the vegetables when the door was slammed open in such haste that it made the pickle jars stacked up inside the door tremble. Everyone looked at Ada, who barged in.

"Have you heard?" she shouted amid her heavy breathing.

"Heard what?" Ann inquired from behind the counter.

"The police have arrested Carl Sutton for double murder, both of Jack and Frank." She smiled a disturbingly improper smile, as a lucky fisher showing off the catch of the day.

"What?" Josie said.

"About time. They should never let that scoundrel be president in the first place," Bella added.

"It's not Nixon, it is Sutton, Carl Sutton!" Ann almost shouted into Bella's ears.

"Oh, Carl; what's with him?"

"I have always known that something has been off with that man, and now he is revealed as the killer he is," Ada said.

"We all know that Carl has his issues, but he is not a killer!" Josie exclaimed.

"If anyone in Kayne is a killer, then Carl is the one. That's what I've always said," Ada continued.

Josie knew that this wasn't only Ada's opinion. If you pushed people in this town to name one person capable of killing, almost all of them would name Carl.

"Maybe he could have killed Frank," Ann objected. "We all know that Carl and Frank didn't get along well together, but why in heaven's name would Carl kill Jack? His only relative and friend. Doesn't make any sense."

Josie sent Ann an approving nod for the support, even though it was a bit half-hearted.

"You never know how these murderers think. I choose to trust the police and they are saying he killed them both."

"That, my dear Ada," Josie shouted and pointed at her, and really didn't know why she called her dear, as there was nothing dear about Ada, at least not right now. "That is a lie." Ada looked at Josie as if she was facing the Spanish inquisition. She was trying to speak, but no words came out of her mouth.

"He is a suspect, and that is all. And I don't want anyone." Josie looked around the store and met the eyes of everyone before she looked back at Ada and continued. "I mean no one to call Carl a killer before judge and jury has spoken – is that clear?"

The silence that followed Josie's fury talk was tangible. Everyone nodded, even Ada.

"Amen, Lieutenant," Ann finally said and broke the silence. But everyone stood there without moving as if they were waiting for Josie's permission to get on with their lives. A few times, Josie had been quite amazed by the authority she possessed by just being the Salvation Army officer in Kayne. She had told herself not to get used to it because she was certain that it wouldn't be so in her next appointment.

"Good," she said and moved toward Ann behind the counter, and the people in the store got back to their business again.

As she came home, Fred was already clearing away their stuff from the hall where they had set up their base.

"I thought you were on your way to the county jail with a suspect."

"So you heard about the arrest," Fred said as he was packing down a laptop.

"News travels fast around here."

"I guess it does. I sent Mr. Sutton with Johnson. I wanted to thank you for your hospitality in person." Fred stopped his work and looked at Josie. "I am, I mean, *we* are very grateful. It's too far to travel back and forth between the city. And setting up an office in a back seat of the car is never a good solution."

"No problem, just glad we could help," Josie said and walked toward the stairs to her apartment. "But you got the wrong guy, by the way."

Josie put the bag of groceries down and turned toward Fred.

"I like that you find the best in everyone, even a guy like Carl, who most people would put their money on as the murderer, but not you. I like that about you," he said and smiled. "But I guess that's up to the jury to decide."

"Is the jury somehow magical?"

"How come?"

# LIKE SMOKE IN THE WIND

Josie took a few steps forward and set her eyes on Fred. "The jury needs something to work on, and that's for you to give them, and you have given them nothing."

"So you come here with your make-believe bogus investigations and want to teach me how to investigate a murder?" Fred shouted. His face was all red. "I'll tell you this, we have all we need; we have motive and opportunity, and we have physical evidence."

"Okay, take me through it, please." Josie softened her tone in an attempt to not anger him even more.

"Motive. He hated Frank, and he was broke and the only one who stands to inherit from Jack."

"Okay, but have you checked how much money Jack had in the bank?"

"No."

"But I can tell you, because I knew this, almost everyone in Kayne knew this, and surely Carl knew this as well. He had a few thousand, between two and three, I believe."

"And?" Fred answered, seemingly unaffected.

"The one thing of real value Carl stood to inherit was the house. Why would he burn down the house? And why now? He had hated Frank for forty years. He had always been broke. Why now?"

"He had opportunity. He had no alibi." Fred sat down on a chair by the table.

"Then you can charge him for all the crimes in the county. He's a loner; he never has an alibi." Josie put her arms up in the air and shook her head. "In the middle of the night, half of Kayne is without an alibi."

Fred nodded. He knew that wasn't his strongest part of the puzzle. "He fixes electrical equipment and would know how to rewire a hot water tank. Not everyone would know that. When the wires that had started the fire were re-examined, they found carbonized newspaper and traces of gasoline. He had switched wires with some that were way too thin and he had wrapped newspapers soaked in gas around them. This made them heat up fast, and a spark would light it up. Not everyone would know that. Then we found an empty jerry can with his prints on it just above Frank's cabin. The gas in it matched the kind used to start the fire." Fred looked at Josie like a card player who has just revealed his final aces.

"So first he is smart and then he is stupid?"

"What do you mean?"

"When he set fire to Jack's house, he thought out a genius plan to burn down a house and make it look like an accident. And mind you, he pulled that one off. You would have believed in the accident theory if it hadn't been for the second fire."

Fred nodded. He had to agree that their first conclusion was an accident and that he would have gotten away with it if it.

"Then, at the second fire, he is so stupid as to leave a vital piece of evidence right by his house?"

"He got sloppy. It happens. The success of the first fire made him overconfident."

"But why throw away his jerry can? He would still need it." Everyone in Kayne had a jerry can in the trunk of their car, except for Josie, who had a smaller can, because a jerry can would take up half the trunk in her tiny Toyota, so she had settled for a much smaller can. Gas stations in this area were so far apart that, for safety reasons, everyone had a can of gas in case they should run out of it. If Carl just threw his away, he would need to buy another one at the first chance. Josie moved slowly toward Fred, pulled out a chair, turned it around and straddled it the same way Fred had done the first time he arrived at the corps, and looked him straight in his eyes.

"You are looking for a murderer who is cold and smart. Carl's mental capacity is wasted by years of alcohol abuse. He simply cannot be the one."

"It's not like on the TV," Fred said. "Most murders committed aren't well-planned."

"Please, Fred, you've got to keep looking."

"For whom?"

"There is a connection with Deirdre Chisholm," Josie said and was immediately reminded of why she had held back on her theory to Fred. He threw his head back and rolled his eyes.

"Why now is the vital question here. Jack talked about Deirdre and that he knew about a secret. A few days later, he was killed. Frank talks about Deirdre being murdered and that he had evidence of it in his home. The same night, he is murdered."

"But why didn't they kill them forty years ago?"

## LIKE SMOKE IN THE WIND

"Please, Fred, you've got to keep looking."

"I am sorry, but I'm sure we've got our guy." Fred got up from his chair and continued packing.

"Just leave the keys on the table before you leave," Josie said. On her way to the stairs, she picked up her grocery bag and disappeared up to her apartment, leaving Fred to himself.

# Chapter 27

"I'll just put on the kettle and make you some tea, honey." Marge was humming in the background. Marge was well into her eighties, but her spirit and vitality made Josie forget her actual age. But every time she came to her house, it was a reminder for her that Marge was an old woman.

"Thanks," Josie replied as her eyes scrolled over the endless rows of ornamental ceramic figures, glass chandeliers and tiny picture frames with distant relatives and neighbor kids on them. Every thank-you card she had ever received had ended up in a frame. Every shelf, every piece of furniture was packed with those things. Josie tried to contemplate the nightmare it would be to dust in her living room.

Josie sat down on the couch close to Marge's favorite chair. She pulled a legal pad and a pen out of her bag and placed it neatly on the table in front of her. She needed to talk to Marge about some practical details of yet another funeral, only a few days after she was done with Jack's. It was, as she had now learned, both about the funeral itself but also the reception after. Marge came out from the kitchen, balancing a tray that she put down on the far end of the table. She gave Josie a cup and placed a teapot on the middle of the table before she placed a cup of coffee at her end. The teapot had still two bags of tea in it, with their labels hanging out on the side. Josie ignored the teapot, and planned to keep ignoring it for at least three minutes until the tea was ready.

"Good thing they caught the one who did it at least," Marge said as she sat down and reached for her coffee. The one – she had known Carl since he was a boy, and now she couldn't even say his name.

"No," Josie replied shortly. She knew if people should pick one amongst them to be charged for murder, or any crime for that matter, it would always be Carl.

"No?" Marge looked at Josie with eyes wide open. "I know you like Carl, but people have died in these fires."

"I just don't believe he did it."

# LIKE SMOKE IN THE WIND

"But the police, they have proof and everything."

"Like what? Of course, he didn't have an alibi. He's living alone up in that cabin of his. He never has an alibi. By the way, what were you doing the night before yesterday? Did you have any alibi?"

"Eh, no," Marge replied, a bit baffled.

"Well, then maybe you did it. Or it might have been me, because I didn't have an alibi. It could be Ann, because Ernie would never wake up if she got out. Shall we go through the whole town and see who actually had an alibi for those two nights?"

"But if he didn't do it, then who did?" Marge said in a demanding tone. Josie got the feeling that she had disrupted the balance. Dealing with two brutal deaths in a quiet small town such as Kayne was hard for the people here. It would have been best if a stranger, an outsider did it. But strangers almost never stopped by Kayne. Carl was the second-best suspect. The alternative was suspecting people they had grown up with, people they thought they trusted. That would take away their sense of security. They maybe even needed to lock doors. Josie waited her out, and stalled by pouring herself some tea, and then took a long sip until she could hear Marge's breathing had returned to normal.

"I don't know," she said finally in her calmest voice. "There are two things I believe the police are missing."

"And that is?"

"The first is that the money motive doesn't stick. Jack was worth more to Carl than the money he owned, which frankly, wasn't a lot."

Marge nodded. The logic was undeniable. Jack was the reason they tolerated Carl as much as they did.

Josie looked at her teacup whilst talking, but she could see Marge in the corner of her eye, giving her a slight nod.

"And... I believe there is a link the police are missing." Josie paused and felt a slight reluctance to bring it up at all. This had been her hunch all along, but if she was wrong, she would be the crazy woman who came up with all these spooky ideas. Then again, they would probably just write it off as an LA kind of thing. Every time she did something that was slightly unorthodox, they would explain it as an LA thing or mumble something about Hollywood. And Marge would probably be the safest person in Kayne to try out her hunch on.

"I believe this somehow is linked to the death of Deirdre Chisholm."

"Deirdre," Marge exclaimed. "But that was an accident, and it's ages ago."

"I'm not saying it wasn't an accident, but there certainly is more to Deirdre than the official account reveals. It has also been the source of bad blood in Kayne all these years."

"Well, that's for sure," Marge said as she nodded her head. "The bad blood between Frank and George. They were best of friends and suddenly they can't stand each other. I don't think anyone else but them knows why, but we all assume it has something to do with Deirdre."

"And now it will never be resolved," Josie said, considering Frank's death.

"Wonder if George will even come to the funeral?" Marge's question was kept hanging unanswered in the air. "But surely none of them would kill Jack over something with Deirdre?"

"But there's more about Deirdre. Remember Jack mistook me for Deirdre? He talked about a secret that he had kept for her."

Marge nodded. No one had forgotten the awkward scene during the flea market.

"Nobody talked about Deirdre, ever; in one year, I haven't heard her be mentioned even once. And suddenly, good old Jack comes talking about an old secret."

"And you think that might be a motive for murder?"

"Depends on the secret."

"No." Marge shrugged. "We don't have that kind of secrets here in Kayne." She straightened up in her chair in a end-of-discussion kind of way.

"How do you know that when it is a secret?"

"But, honey, you can't seriously keep suspecting people to carry around on secrets that they will kill for. After all, this isn't LA."

It had to come eventually, Josie knew that, but she wasn't ready to just leave it at that.

"I know she maybe wasn't the best of girls. But bad things happen to bad people as well, and that doesn't justify..." Josie stopped mid-sentence and just looked at Marge, who sat there with a huge question mark on her face.

"What do you mean not the best of girls? Who have you been talking to?"

Josie swallowed. She obviously didn't know about the pregnancy. Josie assumed no one knew, maybe not even George. She was also not going to break that news to Kayne.

# LIKE SMOKE IN THE WIND

"She was hanging out at the old mill, and I've heard a lot of the mischief, as the home league gossipers called it, was going on up there," Josie said tentatively.

Marge just snorted the reply.

"And George doesn't have one single picture of her in his living room."

"George is a fool. He should cherish her memory instead of tucking it away, and..." Marge was all red-cheeked and kept pointing her finger at Josie. "She was certainly not hanging out at the mill."

Josie had no response. She just sat there and looked at Marge as she regained her natural face color.

"I'm sorry," she said finally.

"Let me just tell you this," Marge said quietly. "If there was anything Deirdre was, it was a good girl. Deirdre was a rare bloom. So nice and kind to everyone. I remember her devotion to the Salvation Army, and we were all so proud to send her off to the training college. She would have put Kayne on the Salvation Army map forever. She was the very best we could ever send."

Josie thought about the application she had withdrawn and figured this was also need-to-know kind of info that they didn't need to know.

"But what about Jack?"

"Oh, Jack was head over heels in love with her." Marge had a tiny smile, and Josie assumed she had a replay from old times in her head. "All the boys were in love with her, but none of them like old Jack. Jack was probably the one who had the best shot also, if it hadn't been that she had her mind set on being an officer."

Josie reached for the teapot.

"Oh, please let me..." Marge said.

"I can handle it, don't worry," Josie answered, and filled up her cup with tea she suspected would be way too strong.

"Of course, I don't know how George would have handled it if that had ever come to be. The richest girl marrying the poorest boy. It was different times back then, you know."

*Tell me about it*, Josie thought as she nodded.

"But old Grandma Sutton, she didn't have much, but everyone, even George, had to respect her."

"Well, maybe we should get back to what we're here for?" Josie said and opened her legal pad. It was the same she had taken notes in for Jack's funeral, so she had to flip through a couple of pages to find an empty one. She would also stop Marge's train of thoughts before she had to listen to one more of these how disappointed Grandma Sutton must have been in Carl.

"Jonathan and Lissie have made some requests for the funeral, but we had a lot more on our plates with Jack's funeral."

"It's, of course, easier with Frank, who has a family. Jack was, after all, alone."

Josie felt again the urge to get the conversation away from Jack and Carl.

"It's only a week between the two funerals. We probably need to ask someone new."

"Well, that's a bit of both. Someone will be offended if they're not asked this time around as well." Marge started listing names, and Josie jotted them down as fast as she could.

"Mrs. Olson will, of course, complain of all she'll have to do."

"Of course," Josie replied. After all, she always complained about something.

"The reason, you see, is that she always needs the extra assurance. So you just need to say that her cakes are so good and she'll be happy."

"I can do that," Josie said. That wouldn't even be a problem. Her cakes were truly marvelous.

"And then we have those who are a bit grumpy because we didn't ask them about Jack's funeral."

Josie continued to write a new list of names, and after the names, she wrote what Marge suggested they should contribute with.

"Now, let's see. How many names do we have now?" Marge said.

"Seventeen."

"That should do it for the food."

Josie nodded.

"For the practical arrangements, we can't use Jonathan, that's obvious, but can we use Jerry, given their parents' history?"

"I don't see why not. George probably won't come, but I believe Jerry would rise above the petty arguments for an occasion like this," Marge said. "And the funeral. How is that going?"

"Jonathan and Lissie have requested some songs. Apart from that, it'll be much of the same, I guess."

"And you did so well last time. I'm sure it will be just fine."

## LIKE SMOKE IN THE WIND

"Jonathan's sisters will come up sometime next week, and I'll talk to them and put together the eulogy then."

# Chapter 28

Josie knew she had been too long in Kayne, when going to Ashville, a town with a total population of fifty-four hundred people, felt like going to a city. It shouldn't be like this, considering she had just recently been in Seattle. The problem, she figured, was that all the time in Seattle she had Kayne on her mind with Deirdre, and Jack's funeral. After her talk with Marge, she had gone up to Carl's house and committed a breaking and entering. Or the door was unlocked, so it was basically just the entering part she had done. She had felt dirty and in the need of a shower after, but it was worth it. She had found what she was looking for. Getting dressed was a trickier part. Being an officer in the Salvation Army, you spend little time pondering outfits. It was usually the uniform. She had landed on the uniform this time as well, but she had been uncertain. It felt like she was misusing the Salvation Army and her position as an officer, but the uniform usually goes a long way in opening doors. If she was right in her suspicions, she could defend her use of the uniform, but would feel a bit guilty if it all was just a part of her imagination. As her car came down from the mountain, she got a brief glimpse of the ash forest that gave Ashville its name. Then the road that cut straight through it all the way to the town. Seconds later, she was inside the forest, and apart from the road, she only saw the tree-line on both sides of the road.

Ashville was a simple town to figure out. First Street, or Main Street, as some preferred to call it, had all the stores. Second Street had the schools at one end, and small businesses in the other. There you could find a garage, a carpentry and plumbers and such. Josie always wondered how these businesses kept in business year after year. After all, her impression was that people around here fixed everything themselves. If their clutch broke down, they needed a clutch, not an auto mechanic, and if a pipe broke, they needed a pipe, not a plumber. Of course, Josie needed all those, but she couldn't keep them all afloat on her salary. She understood that selling parts was probably their primary income.

# LIKE SMOKE IN THE WIND

Her first stop in Ashville took her to First Street, and this stop she had not taken into consideration when she went in full uniform. She stopped outside one of the larger stores. It said Ashville Grocery, but on the side, there was another door with a smaller sign that said 'Liquor and Wine' on it. They separated the alcohol department of the grocery store from the main store with its own door. At entry, a bell would ring and one clerk from the grocery store would come over. Josie felt highly uncomfortable entering the liquor store in a Salvation Army uniform. She found a picture on her phone of two empty bottles from Carl's place. The bottles had a golden label saying 'brandy.' She easily found the bottles, except these contained a brown liquid. They weren't the most expensive bottles, but they were almost three times the price of the cheapest bottle of liquor. That someone gave Carl some money, knowing that he was almost always broke, wasn't unthinkable. That alcoholics weren't the most rational with money was also true. But for Carl, who almost always drank moonshine, just going to the liquor store was a stretch. Buying two bottles for the same as he could get six for the same price. Sure, he could feel rich and liked to taste something fancy, but buying two bottles revealed a motivation to get drunk, not to taste something fancy. But if Carl hadn't done it, then maybe someone had gone out of their way to frame Carl, considering his jerry can was at the scene. That would be easier if Carl was so drunk, he couldn't remember what he did that night. Josie's theory was that someone provided him with the alcohol.

"May I help you, miss?" the clerk said, arriving from the main store. She was a woman not much older than Josie, probably somewhere in her thirties.

"Sure," Josie said. She pulled the brandy from the shelf and went over to the counter. "I'm sorry, but I'm not buying."

"I thought as much," she answered, referring to the uniform.

"I need to know if someone bought two of these bottles yesterday or the day before?"

The clerk said nothing. She was probably hesitating, not knowing if it was right to reveal her customers.

"I wouldn't ask if it wasn't important."

"Tuesday afternoon," she said shortly.

"Do you know who it was? Can you describe him?" Josie asked. She wanted to ask if he looked like a hobo, but remembered that on Tuesday, Carl didn't look like a hobo. Newly washed in his suit, he looked quite good.

"Not a regular. It was a man, an old man."

An old man could be almost half the population of Kayne. She remembered she had taken a picture of Carl newly washed in his new suit. She wished to preserve the image of Carl looking that fresh. She scrolled down the pictures on her phone and showed the lady behind the counter.

"No, not him."

Josie was happy to be back in her car and could roll out of the parking spot. She hoped not too many people had seen the Salvation Army lieutenant in the liquor store. It wasn't much of a description she had gotten, but she got her phone number and could send her a picture if she needed to.

Her second stop at Ashville took her past the schools and to a street called Cedar Street. It was a residential area with small houses, all with a fair-sized garden. All the houses had their white picket fence and a well-cared-for lawn. House number thirty-four was a bright yellow house. It had a double garage, but no cars in the driveway. Usually, cars stood in the driveway because the garage was filled up with everything else. She parked out in the street and walked up the driveway to the door. She must have been observed as she parked because the door was opened before she reached to ring the doorbell.

"Please, come in, miss..." The 'miss' was stretched out as she was waiting for the name to appear out of the blue.

"Facundo, but you can call me Josie. You are Mrs. Abigail, I suppose," Josie said as she entered. Ms. Carrington had married and become the posh Mrs. Abigail. It had taken Josie some time to figure it out, because she was reluctant to involve too many in the search of the mysterious top five list. Mrs. Abigail had gray hair, but her smooth skin made her look like she was in the middle of her forties, not pushing sixty. Josie followed the lady into the living room and they sat down in two brown leather recliners placed by the window overlooking the garden.

"I must say, I'm a bit intrigued by your request to help you hunt down some old demons."

Josie smiled. She wouldn't say too much to prevent putting her off, but if she said too little, Mrs. Abigail might not even bother to give information.

# LIKE SMOKE IN THE WIND

"I don't know how to put this, but there is some bad blood between some people and I fear that a crime has been committed, maybe even several."

"I really don't know how I can help. I've hardly ever been to Kayne."

"This goes way back, back to your senior year in high school. And remember, whatever you choose to tell me stays between you and me."

"Sure."

"Some boys back then had something they called the top five list of girls, and you were on it."

"It's probably not the first time boys ranked girls."

"Someone bragged about sleeping with you, and I wonder if it happened and if it was voluntary?"

Mrs. Abigail looked down and shook her head.

"I fear this is not my brightest moment. He had a car, he worked at the auto-shop. He came from the big city. Own car, money, and dressed like people we only saw on TV ticked a lot of boxes for a young and shallow girl." Mrs. Abigail looked like she had a hard time connecting with the eighteen-year-old version of herself. "He was pushy all right, but I let it happen. It was a Wednesday afternoon, in the back of his car. I regretted it immediately. Probably he did too. I never heard from him again."

Josie suspected that regret had nothing to do with her not hearing anything from Oscar again, but she chose not to tell her.

"I'm sorry I couldn't help you, but it wasn't rape," she said.

"Oh, you've helped me. The truth is always helpful."

Josie bade Mrs. Abigail good-bye and got back to her car and looked at the next address, the third and last stop on her trip.

# Chapter 29

She drove back on Second Street and passed the auto shop where Oscar once worked. He later moved on to work at the dam, probably helped to get the job by George. The road called Dr. Smith Street was clearly at the dodgier end of Ashville. All the gardens were the same size as on Cedar Street, but not as well-kept. The houses were smaller and far more beat-up as well. She parked outside number 53. An old white wooden building that had not seen fresh paint for at least a couple of decades. Roof tiles were coming off, and the chimney lacked a few stones. It didn't seem to bother Maddie Mackey. She was all smiles when she greeted Josie and invited her in.

"Do you want something to drink? Hot or cold?"

"A cup of tea, please."

Despite the ragged exterior, it was nice and clean inside. The furniture was old, but not older than what she had back in Kayne. In one corner, there were some colorful plastic toys; tractors and trucks seemed to be the all-around theme.

"So, here's some tea," she said as she came out balancing a tray. She placed a cup of tea in front of Josie and a cup of coffee in front of herself.

"Thank you," Josie replied. "Let me guess, you've got a grandson." Josie gestured to the toys in the corner.

"Two, in fact. Matt is five and Luke is three," she said and was bursting with pride. "I look after them when my daughter is working the evening shifts. She's a nurse." Maddie was no less proud of her daughter, Josie thought.

"I enjoy having the kids around. There's so much life in them."

"Kids are lovely," Josie said and took a sip of her tea. Maddie took a sip of her coffee and it all came to a short silence.

"So, how can I help you with those old demons of yours?" Maddie finally said and smiled.

Josie hesitated. It was an awkward and uncomfortable question to ask. To see how Mrs. Abigail reacted to her question didn't make it any easier. She felt she couldn't pop out with a question like that. But Maddie Mackey seemed to be one of those people not too fond of beating around the bush. Josie noticed she was getting impatient, and she knew she couldn't stall anymore.

"In your senior year at high school, someone up in Kayne bragged about sleeping with you. I wondered if that happened and if it was with your consent?"

Maddie's smile faded, and she looked down into her cup. It was like a dark cloud of terrible memories that she had fought keeping at bay now suddenly appeared in her face. Josie thought she would throw her out, but nothing happened. She just sat there and stared at her coffee.

"It was a Saturday evening, I was in..." she said. Her voice cracked, and she stopped to wipe a tear from the corner of her eye. "I was in Kayne, hanging with some friends. I should have called for my father to come and get me, but Oscar offered to drive me home."

Josie nodded to affirm that she listened, but said nothing. She was fidgeting with her fingers. This wasn't a story Maddie was used to telling.

"He just wanted to show me something, and he showed me the mill. It was closed down with some planks, but he used a crowbar and removed the planks and we stepped inside."

*Kayne March 1978*

"Come on," Oscar said, grabbing her by her hand and pulling her inside the dark mill.

"Is this allowed?" Maddie said with a concerned voice. "I heard it was closed down."

"Don't worry; no one will ever know." He pulled her further in through the narrow hallway that took them past the mill wheel. "Here we can do whatever we want, and no one will ever know," Oscar said and stroked her gently on her cheek.

"I just want to go home," she said and slowly moved toward the door.

"Why the rush? It's still early," Oscar said, playing it cool.

"Please, Oscar, just take me home."

"Let's chill a bit, you and I." Oscar laid his arm over her shoulders.

"You promised you'd take me home," Maddie said.

"No," he said and pulled her back and pushed her down into some hay that lay in the corner. "If I'm going to do you a favor, you need to do me one first." His voice had changed from soft to hard, and it scared Maddie.

"Please don't," she pleaded.

"Don't worry," he said. His voice had turned back to being soft. But Maddie lay there paralyzed by fear as he slowly unbuttoned her blouse.

"I got away. I pushed him away." Josie could hear a new strength in her voice. "And I ran. I was half naked, but I just ran. So glad no one saw me. I was almost back in Kayne when I dared to stop and get fully dressed. I went to Lissie and her father drove me home."

"Did you tell him what happened?"

"No, but I guessed he knew something bad had happened."

"Did you tell anyone?"

"I'm telling you now," she said and burst out in tears. Josie moved over and kneeled beside her. Then she gently removed her cup and placed it on the table. Josie held the lady who had carried this awful secret to herself for over four decades. They sat like this for several minutes. The hard floor was numbing Josie's knees, but she felt it would be wrong to get up while Maddie held on to her so hard. It felt like an eternity when Maddie finally let go and wiped the tears off her face with the sleeve of her blouse arm. Josie just sat there kneeling on the floor before her. She had no feeling in her knees and knew she would struggle to get up.

"And yes, he bragged about it. Even though he never got to complete the rape, he bragged about it like we had done it. It was like being raped all over again."

"Do you remember what year or maybe even month this was?"

"Sure, March eleventh, seventy-eight. I'm afraid I'll never forget it."

Josie got up on weary legs and she had to walk a few steps to get the circulation running again.

"Thank you, you have been most helpful," Josie said as she was leaving.

## LIKE SMOKE IN THE WIND

"No, I should thank you. It did me good to finally tell someone. Having someone that believed me," Maddie replied. "Because you do believe me, don't you?"

"Sure I believe you," Josie replied.

# Chapter 30

The hardware store was the largest of the stores in Kayne. It provided tools and spare parts for any thinkable and unthinkable task. People in rural Spokane were handy, and fixed everything they could fix and a lot of things they weren't qualified to fix. Josie looked through all the different locks, and couldn't really decide which ones would fit her doors. It was Marge's loss of her key that made her think of it. Not because she thought Marge's key had fallen into the wrong hands. But because there probably were a dozen old keys lying around in Kayne to her apartment door. She had once found a key list, or at least an attempt of a key list, but none of the keys were signed in again and it hadn't been updated for decades.

"Do you need any help?" Lissie had appeared in front of her without making a single sound, or at least not one that Josie had heard.

"I'm thinking of changing the lock to the apartment, but I'm uncertain which one it is."

"Is it broken?"

"No, but it's so old that I don't think there is any control over the keys anymore."

"Then it's a cheap insurance," Lissie said. "The safest thing is to take it out and bring it over. Just remove the pins from the handle and unscrew these screws, and it will come out." Lissie pointed at the screw holes in the lock Josie already held in her hand. Josie said nothing, even though she knew how to change a lock. When she was in LA, they actually considered her quite handy, but out here, she was just a city-girl with ten thumbs.

"How are things going with you, by the way?"

"You know, it's a lot with the funeral and all, but we're at least glad it seems like they've caught the guy."

Josie didn't comment. She still couldn't believe Carl had done it, and certainly could not see how he would have any more motive than any other. But she couldn't say that to Lissie, at least not now, only days before she was leading the funeral of Frank. And then it was her gut feeling that it was somehow connected with Deirdre, but how was impossible to prove.

"Lissie, you'll have to take a day at a time," Josie said, and focused on addressing Lissie directly. Most people talked about Jonathan's loss, and whenever they mentioned it to Lissie, it was always the plural for you. Like Lissie was an invader in the family, with no emotions of her own in this matter.

"It's at least good having my hands full. It makes the days go by easier."

"If it helps, I can always provide you with some extra chores after the funeral is over to make sure you still have your hands full," Josie said with a smile and an ironic tone in her voice. Still, the serious message behind the joke was that she acknowledged that the mourning wasn't over when the funeral was done.

"Oh, that's super nice of you," she said with a smile. "But I think Frank has beaten you to it. We'll have to go through all his stuff up in the attic."

"His stuff? But didn't that burn in the fire?"

"When he moved up to the cabin, he brought only what he needed. The rest of his junk, which includes papers from the store dating as long as ninety years back, is still sitting up in the store's attic." Lissie sighed. "Most of it is junk, but I guess we'll have to go through it."

"Sure, but you mean all the stuff he stacked away was stacked away in your attic, not his?"

"Yeah," she answered while raising her eyebrows and arching her head back as if to say, *wasn't that what I just told you?* Josie remembered Becker's word on taking the chances when they presented themselves.

"Lissie, I know this is an odd request, but..." she said, and felt a need to rephrase. "I talked to Frank only a few days before he died. It's related to something entirely different. He told me about a paper up in the attic that could help me understand something." Josie paused and could see Lissie waited for the question, even though she probably had already guessed it. "Can I look through his papers to see if I find it?"

"Sure, when?"

"Now," Josie said and nodded eagerly.

"Okay, but it's desperately dusty up there."

It was desperately dusty up there. As Lissie turned on the light, the dust danced in the faint shimmer.

"There's not much light here," she said and pointed at the single light bulb hanging from the roof in the middle of the attic. "But you can borrow this flashlight." Lissie handed her a flashlight she had brought with her from the store. Josie recognized it from the search party for Jack. Lissie and Jonathan had probably emptied their storage of flashlights that night. Now they had a bunch of flashlights they couldn't sell because they were slightly used.

"Thanks," Josie replied.

"This is our stuff," she said and pointed to a small heap close to the door. Mostly empty suitcases and boxes with clothes, by the look of it. "Then Frank's private stuff is on his right, and stuff on the left is from the store."

"Oh my, he had just as much here as he had in his cabin."

"I told you, good luck," Lissie replied. "I'll be down in the store if you need me."

"Thanks a lot, Lissie," Josie replied. Lissie was already on her way down the stairs, leaving Josie alone in the dimly lit and dusty room. She turned on the flashlight. It was a powerful light, stronger than the headlight she used while jogging after dark. She guessed that went with the territory. If you run a hardware store, you don't have bad flashlights. The light scanned the entire room. The section with Frank's stuff was by far the biggest one. But on the bright side, she knew she was looking for a paper, so the furniture she didn't need to bother with, only the boxes. Of course, she had to move most of the furniture because the boxes were all behind them. She walked slowly over the floor. The planks creaked as she put her weight on them. It was smaller furniture, like chairs, smaller tables and dressers. Still, moving them away from the boxes made her sweat. It took almost a half an hour to move all the furniture well away from the boxes. She counted thirty-nine cardboard boxes, and none of them had any description of the content. The worst part was that she really didn't know what she was looking for. She knew it was some kind of paper, and she knew it probably was from around seventy-eight, maybe seventy-seven.

She picked up the first box. It was thoroughly taped with a brown tape. She realized that a knife would come in handy, but she had no intention of going to find a knife now. She used a key and ripped up the tape. The contents of the first box was at first a disappointment. It was ornamental figures in glass

## LIKE SMOKE IN THE WIND

and ceramics. Josie shoved it to the side and found the next ones. It contained tablecloths, and it was then it dawned upon her that this probably wasn't such a big job after all because most of the boxes didn't contain any papers. She had reached box number thirteen when it was something with papers in it. It was old binders. She picked one up to check the date and found it was really hard to flip through a binder and hold the flashlight at the same time. The light from the light bulb in the center of the room wasn't nearly enough for her to read by. At least not in the corner with the boxes. She got up, found the best chair and positioned it under the light, and placed a small table in front of it. Then she pulled the box over to the chair and sat down, pulling out one binder after the other. They all seemed to contain businesslike letters and receipts. Good thing they were all easy to date. She looked at the beginning, the end, and once somewhere in the middle. If the dates were consistent, and they were, then she assumed that all the letters would be within that timeframe. The first box stretched back to the mid-eighties. The second box with papers was number twenty-six. Here she found the seventy-five to early seventy-nine binder. This was the binder she had to go thoroughly through. It was papers; it was from the right period of time, but she still wasn't sure what she looked for. But all this time, she had thought that she would know it when she saw it. Now she wasn't so sure. Anything concerning the Chisholms she read carefully, like one letter where he informed George that Mr. Olson had ordered a new bumper for his car, because according to Jack, Oscar had stolen the old one to fit on his car, or a note stating that George had to bail on a fishing trip because he had urgent matter in Spokane to take care of. The papers were crisp and yellowish. But nothing had a fairly remote connection to Deirdre Chisholm.

"Nothing, absolutely nothing," she spoke out loud as she put the binder back into the box and kicked the box to the side. She looked at the even neater pile of boxes on the left side of the attic belonging to the store. What could possibly be in those papers that could incriminate anyone or even shed light over anything? she thought. Still, it was better than going through a bunch of old letters. The good thing about this was that these boxes were neatly arranged by year and it was written on top of them what it was. She found two boxes: one said "Books and Reports" and the other one said "Orders and Receipts."

Josie pulled the "Order and Receipts" one over to the chair. This one had been staying here since seventy-eight and the level of dust was in a whole new

141

league. Josie wiped off the dust with her hand before opening it. It whirled up a cloud of dust and caused Josie to sneeze several times. The order inside was perfect. There was a binder for each month. She started with April, since the fire was in late April. Then she went through every binder until September. Maybe it was earlier, she thought, and pulled the one for March. It was all the same, nothing that you wouldn't expect from a hardware store. Receipt for paint to F. Olson, an exhaust system for a Chevrolet pickup ordered for E. Mitchum, that had to be Ernie, she thought. Changing a lock for G. Chisholm, a Schlage lock changed by Jack Sutton, and keys signed out to G. Chisholm. Fixing a leak for Miss Harriet, work and two gaskets. The list just went on and on. Everyone in Kayne used the hardware store.

"Are you okay up there?" Lissie shouted up the steep stairs to the attic.

"Yeah, I'm fine," she replied.

"Do you want some lunch?" Lissie's head peeked up in the stairway. Josie had hoped she wouldn't come up and see what mess she had made.

"Sorry about the mess. I will tidy up after me."

"No problem. Come and get something to eat."

"You got dust all over," Lissie said as Josie climbed down the stairs. She took her index finger over her forehead and showed Josie the dust gathered on her finger.

"Sweat and dust, not the best combination."

She had bought bread rolls from next door, the same Josie had brought the day Frank died. This time around, there was no uncomfortable inspector making her leave before she was done eating.

A half an hour later, she was back up again. With fresh energy, the task didn't look as daunting anymore. Lissie had sent with her a bottle of water to clear her throat from all the dust, so she breathed lighter as well. She returned to Frank's personal boxes. The last boxes contained letters and other more personal stuff. It made sense that these boxes came last. They probably stood here before he packed and moved for the cabin. It was letters between Frank and his wife. The earliest was probably before they got married. None of them was even close to the time period she was looking for. Then there were a lot of children drawings that Jonathan and his sisters had signed in a preschool manner. She looked through the Christmas cards. It seemed they regularly had gotten Christmas cards from the Chisholms. It didn't stop when George's wife

# LIKE SMOKE IN THE WIND

died. They just changed the sender to George and family. They stopped in seventy-seven. That was the last card they had sent. It proved nothing about the death of Deirdre, but it told her that the disagreement between George and Frank had something to do with Deirdre.

But that was it. Nothing else than a broken line of Christmas cards. Josie sighed again. She had been up there for hours, and nothing to show for it. She looked at the pile of boxes and furniture that had been neatly stacked together. Now they lay spread out all over the floor. Sliding exhausted down on the floor, she knew she had to tidy up after herself. She just needed a brief rest and a moment to cope with the disappointment of not finding anything useful. She took a sip of water and looked at the dust dancing around the single light bulb.

"Josie, you're such a fool!" she said out loud, before she, with newfound vigor, went back to the boxes she had gone through before lunch. Knowing what she looked for, it was a simple task, and minutes later, she held up the piece of paper, Frank's evidence.

# Chapter 31

"Lissie, I need to talk to you." Josie popped into the store. Her hair was gray from all the dust up in the attic.

"One second, Josie," Lissie said. She was just about finished with a customer. She put a wrench, a padlock and a pack of smoke detectors into a plastic bag and handed it to the customer. Josie figured they sold quite a few smoke detectors nowadays. She realized she should have checked the smoke detectors in the Salvation Army as well. They were probably old.

"Josie, what can I do for you?"

"Can we talk in private?" Josie wiped the dusty hair away from her face. Normally, in the state she was, she wouldn't see anyone, but head right back home for a long shower. It was even worse than it had been after the flea market.

"Sure, we can step inside the office," she replied. "Jonathan, I'm leaving you alone in the store for a minute," she shouted down to Jonathan, who was helping someone in the tool section. They stepped inside the tiny office where Lissie used to sit doing the books.

"So, did you find what you were looking for?"

"Sure, and now I need to ask you a favor."

"Of course. What?"

"I need you and Jonathan to go away from Saturday to Sunday. Go after the shop closes and check into a hotel in Spokane or something."

"Why?" she said with an air of dismay.

If that troubled her, the next piece of information probably would freak her out, she thought. Figuring out what to say and how to say it was always a trick you never knew the answer to before it was too late. Never mind, she thought, and told her straight out.

"Because someone will try to burn down your house."

"What? Why?"

"Because of what I found. Frank was killed because he knew about this." Josie held up the receipt she had found. "His cabin was burnt down to eliminate

# LIKE SMOKE IN THE WIND

this." Josie put the receipt back in her pocket without revealing what it was. "And when the killer realizes that it's in your attic, not in Frank's cabin, he will try to burn down this house as well."

"No, hold on just a minute. Carl is in prison." Lissie shook her head and held up her hands. Then she turned away from Josie and faced the bookshelf behind the desk. She turned back to Josie and then away again. Like she was going in a circle, but the office was so tiny that she ended up spinning around.

"No, no, no," she kept saying as she was turning from side to side. "He won't kill anymore and he won't start any more fires. The police made sure of that."

"No, Carl didn't do it. Carl was framed as the murderer."

"Are you sure?" The disappointment in her voice had nothing to do with Carl not being a killer, but rather that someone else – someone they knew even better – was the killer. "And he knows that the paper wasn't at Frank's?"

"No, that we'll have to tell him." Josie tried to smile casually, as if she suggested something entirely ordinary.

"Now, why would we do that?"

"Because one day he'll find out anyway and it's better that we catch him sooner than later, or maybe even too late."

"Do you think he will kill us?" At this point, Lissie sounded scared. It guilted Josie a bit, but at least it meant she was getting through to her.

"I don't think so. Jack and Frank died because they knew something. You don't know anything. You still don't," Josie said and patted the pocket with the receipt. Of course, he had already killed two people and he probably wouldn't hesitate if he felt it was necessary. That was why Josie thought it best to give the killer a chance to burn down the house without Lissie and Jonathan inside it.

"But can't we wait until after the funeral?"

"Sure, I guess that's possible, but that means he will come to your funeral and he will offer you his condolences."

Lissie shuddered from the idea. "But why do we need to let him burn down the house?"

"I'll make sure the police stop him, but we need the conclusive evidence."

Lissie thought long and hard. This was not an easy decision for her. Finally, she bit her teeth together and placed her fist on the desk. "Ok, let's do it. I'll talk to Jonathan."

"It's one more thing. After closing, you should eat at the diner. While there, you must talk about Jonathan taking you to Spokane. Tell them you have decided to relax a few days before you go through all of Frank's stuff that's in your attic."

Lissie nodded.

"Don't forget to mention that he has a ton of papers lying there."

"Sure, I can do that."

"And try to tell as many as you can in the store tomorrow."

"I'll do what I can."

The problem with being impulsive is facing the consequences later. Like calling the police in Spokane and telling them she had set up a trap for a killer. A killer they already had imprisoned as well. Her hands were sweaty as she held on to her phone. He could be on his way home from the office now. Off to something he'd been looking forward to all week. He would not be happy, that was for sure. She went through her contacts and found Fred's number, which she saved after he had called her.

"Are you out of your freaking mind?"

The conversation had started much nicer. As she called, he had been pleased to hear from her, or at least so he told her. But as she told her about her plans, his 'hm-m's' had become worryingly louder.

"That's the stupidest thing I've ever heard. The police don't lay traps; that's just in the movies."

"In all fairness, the police didn't lay this trap either. I did."

"You sure did. I can't believe what you were thinking." She could hear Fred was walking in circles at the other end.

"Fred, just listen."

"Inspector Becker, please."

"You're that mad?" Josie cringed at the thought. *It's never like this in the books.*

"Yes, I'm that mad."

"Okay, listen to me, Inspector Becker."

"Listening," he said. "And this better be good."

# LIKE SMOKE IN THE WIND

"If you are absolutely sure that Carl is the one that was behind these fires, then you have nothing to worry about."

"What do you mean?"

"That there is no arsonist murderer on the loose in Kayne." Josie treaded nervously around her living room. "Then all that happens is that the Meadowses get themselves a weekend in Spokane, which I believe they need. And I'll be lying a night in the bushes waiting for nobody to show up."

Josie waited long enough to give Fred a chance to raise his concerns. But Fred was not jumping in to raise doubt over his own suspect.

"Of course, if I got it right, then you'd better hope I'm able to stop him."

"Why?"

"Because it would be highly embarrassing for the Spokane Sheriff Department if there's a third fire in Kayne in less than three weeks, and," she said and paused for the dramatic effect. "The police were tipped about it."

"So, this is a tip now?" Fred still sounded furious. "Because it feels more like a blackmail."

Josie was about to answer when she heard a crash on the other end.

"Hello – hello!" Josie said, but no one answered. She realized that Inspector Becker had thrown his phone away. She could hear him in the background rambling about and talking to himself. It wasn't the nicest of language he was using. Still mad, Josie concluded. She stayed on the phone. She had no intention of giving up. Things were already set in motion and she needed it to play out, and she needed Fred to come along. She timed her watch. She wasn't talking to him anymore, so he had no provocations at the time. That was good news. It meant that adrenaline was dropping, and she knew the halftime for adrenaline was about three minutes. So in about three minutes' time, she assumed he would pick up the phone and talk to her. She reckoned it probably would be a better strategy to be humble, so she didn't have to wait another three minutes.

Three minutes is an awful long time when you sit and stare into a phone. The seconds that went over three minutes were even longer, but at three minutes and fourteen seconds, she could hear the phone being picked up again.

"You still there, Josie?" Fred spoke in a milder voice this time around.

"I'm sorry, Inspector Becker. It was foolish of me."

147

"Yes, it was," he said. Then there was a pause. Josie reckoned he was still quite mad at her. "How sure are you?"

"Very. Ninety-nine percent."

"I hoped you'd say a hundred and ten."

"People that say hundred and ten are either bad at math or are exaggerating. Ninety-nine percent means certain, but realistic."

"Okay, let's say you're right. The true murderer will come and burn down their house because you made him believe that the evidence that was lost in Frank's cabin actually was in the attic of the hardware store. Why would he believe your bluff?"

"Because it isn't a bluff. The papers actually were in the attic of the hardware store, except now they are in my pocket."

"But if you have the proof, then why do you need to catch him in the act?"

"Because it proves Deirdre was murdered. It sure ties him to it, but I don't believe it's conclusive. And it doesn't link him to the recent fires more than it's a strong motive."

"Let's say I believe you. I can't just walk into the sheriff's office and demand a night's stakeout. That's not how these things work."

"So what then?"

"I'm off duty this weekend. I'll talk to some of the other guys that also are off for the weekend."

"Thanks, Fred, you're the best."

"But here's the deal. We are coming to make sure you are safe, that's all. So you'd better serve us a great supper when we arrive. We need coffee and food for the night, and a breakfast when it's over."

"Sure, I can do that. It'll be a breakfast you'll remember for years."

"Are you really that good a cook, or is it the guilt talking?"

"Clearly the guilt, but I'll do my best."

Fred had called back when Josie came out of the shower. She wrapped the towel around her and picked up the phone.

"Hello, Fred."

## LIKE SMOKE IN THE WIND

"Hi, I've got two colleagues to partner up with me. Harry, who has been here with me, and Don, a young fellow."

"That's great. Thank you, Fred." She yanked the phone between her ear and her shoulder as she reached for an extra towel to throw on the floor. Stepping out of the shower soaking wet had made the old linoleum on the floor slippery.

"Just hope it's not in vain."

"I promise you it won't be."

They hung up and Josie followed her own advice to Lissie and ate at the diner. It would work as a test if her plan worked, if the gossip had started to spread. She needed to make sure she arrived after the Meadowses to test if they were talking about it. And by 'they,' she really meant Peggy. That gave her time to fix her hair and even put on some makeup. She didn't use much makeup, but sometimes it felt good to posh up a little bit. She got into some clean clothes and was ready for the local diner.

# Chapter 32

"Mr. Bowers, how are you?" Jonathan asked. The bell hanging on the door of the hardware store rang, and Oscar Bowers stepped inside.

"I'm fine, thanks," he replied. "I guess I'm out for what most people need these days."

"Smoke detectors?"

"That's right, if you've still got any left." With the two fires in the town, everyone now checked their smoke detectors and fire extinguishers. As always, they would buy it at Frank's in Kayne. Buying them in Ashville would be considered disloyal.

"Well." Jonathan dragged out his answer. "Your house isn't the biggest, so I don't think you need the interconnected ones. Then I might just help you." Jonathan walked toward the shelf and picked up a square white box. "How many do you need?"

"Two, I guess."

"That would be about right." Jonathan picked up another one and walked back to the counter. "Do you need batteries as well?"

"Sure."

Jonathan found two batteries from behind the counter and started tapping it into the register.

"Anything else?"

Oscar shook his head.

"That will be $36.98." Jonathan started putting the items in a plastic bag while Oscar reached for his wallet.

"Jonathan, dear, do you have any clothes that need washing before we go?" Lissie broke in.

"No," Jonathan answered, tired of answering the endless lines of questions regarding the trip.

## LIKE SMOKE IN THE WIND

"Jonathan is taking me to Spokane for the weekend. After the weekend, when his sisters arrive for the funeral, we will have to go through all of Frank's stuff that he left in our attic. There are a ton of papers there."

"That I can imagine," Oscar replied.

"So Jonathan thought a weekend off could do us good." Lissie sparkled when she talked about the trip to anyone who bothered to listen to her. The rumor was that she was quite excited about going away for a weekend. But no one found that odd; after all, they couldn't recall the Meadowses doing anything like that ever. Jonathan wasn't so sure about this imminent threat those women had cooked together. He suspected it all was a trick to make him take Lissie on a weekend trip to the city. But he played along as best as he could.

"Sounds like a good idea. You two have fun," Oscar said and smiled his cheesiest smile as he took his bag and walked out of the store. He almost crashed into Josie on his way out.

"Hello, Ms. Josie," Jonathan said. "Are you here to buy something, or have you just come to conspire with my wife on future holiday plans for me?"

"Relax, old man, you'll love it."

"I've told everyone I've met, just as you said," Lissie said, and smiled. Josie could see that she was actually looking forward to going away.

"Good," Josie replied. "Inspector Fred Becker and two other police officers from Spokane will watch your house throughout the night."

"Oh," Lissie said, and her smile faded. Suddenly, the reality of why they were going away kicked in.

"That sounds reassuring," Jonathan shot in.

"But actually, I am here to buy something." Josie smiled at Jonathan.

"You should buy a lot to make up for all the money you cost me on your last visit," Jonathan said and tried to put up a grumpy face, but it didn't persuade anyone.

"I need new smoke detectors for the Army."

"It's a large building, so I will recommend the interconnected ones," Jonathan said. "They are made so that if one goes off, the rest will go off too. So if a fire starts in the basement, then the ones in your apartment will go off as well."

"Sounds okay. How many do you think I need?" Jonathan had been going to the Army his entire life and knew the building. As did, of course, almost everyone in Kayne. That always made things easier when she needed something.

"I'll recommend six. My most popular comes in three packs for a fair price." His prices would always be quite higher than the ones in the superstores in Spokane, but if you added a two-hour drive to Spokane into the price, Jonathan's prices were a bargain. And the service was unbeatable.

"Then I'll take six."

"Of course, I'm sold out for the moment, but I ordered more yesterday. I'll expect them early next week," Jonathan said and wrote the order down in a notebook.

"We are selling a lot in fire security these days," Lissie shot in.

"Too bad we need a tragedy to wake up, and in this case, two."

Josie said, "Enjoy your trip, and thanks for doing this."

"Sure, you're welcome," Lissie said with a convincing smile. Jonathan smiled as well, but not as convincing.

"You really need to get yourself a bigger car," Fred said as Josie came out of her car. They had both parked outside the Ashville High School. Fred had told her to come for them. Kayne was so tiny that a strange car would raise suspicions.

"I'm glad to see you too," Josie replied. She walked over and gave him a hug before she greeted the two others.

"I didn't say I was glad to see you."

"Still mad?"

Fred nodded. "In the future, leave police work to the police."

"I'm sorry. Shall we go?"

"Sure." Fred nodded to the other two, and they loaded two large black bags into her trunk. They barely fit in her trunk and covered much of her rear view.

"What's all that?"

"Surveillance equipment, only the most basic," Harry said. They got into her car. Fred was shotgun and the other two rode in the back.

"We will hide out in your apartment for at least an hour until it's dark enough, and the streets are quiet enough to do an inspection."

"Inspection of what?"

## LIKE SMOKE IN THE WIND

"The most likely scenarios for an arsonist, what side of the house he will set on fire and so on."

It was dark when they arrived, and Kayne didn't really have a night life during the weekends. The youngsters eager to go to a party or something always drove down to Ashville, or even further. They met a few of them along the way. Some of them the police officers probably would like to pull over for reckless driving and speeding. Josie parked outside the Army, got out of the car, and opened the door to the corps before the police officers got out. They were out of the car and into the hall in a matter of seconds. While Josie made them supper, they spread the contents of their bags all over her living room and tested the cameras and screens. The police officers all went into a work mode, concentrating on the job. The jokes and banter were off. They only talked about things related to the stakeout. During supper, they all sat in silence. It was an awkward mood.

"It's time," Fred said. It was a quarter to midnight. They had deemed it highly unlikely that the arsonist would attempt anything before midnight. And they needed to wait as long as possible to avoid being spotted as they set up the surveillance. They started by setting up one camera in Josie's living room window overlooking the main street. Then Don took two cameras and headed down the main street while Fred and Harry took the rest of the equipment to the back of the house and into Marge's garden. Don mounted one facing the front of the hardware store. He planted it in a tree on the other side of the road. Then he went around the corner of the hardware store where the stairs up to Jonathan and Lissie's apartment were. He put one camera to monitor that side of the house. He found Fred in the corner of Marge's garden.

"All set?" Don asked.

"I'm pulling up the cameras now. Harry is mounting one camera overlooking the front of Marge's house." Marge's garden was surrounded by a large hedge, so they were well covered. There was no way an arsonist in the backyard of the hardware store could spot them. The only exception was if he entered through Marge's garden, then he would come upon them from behind. The camera Harry mounted overlooking the front of Marge's house was their insurance if that should happen.

153

"It seems they're working properly," Fred said as one after the other of the cameras popped up on the screen. "Looking good," Fred said as the images from the cameras kept popping up on the screen.

"Don, take a look at this." Don looked over Fred's shoulder as he pointed to the camera overlooking the front of the store. "Wouldn't it be better if you turned it slightly right, so it covers the entrance to the apartment as well?"

"Sure, I'll go. Just tell me when it's where you want it."

A minute later, Don was by the tree and he adjusted the last camera into the right position. Fred took a knife and cut down some branches of the hedge, giving them a visual through the hedge.

They left Josie in the apartment. She had tried to persuade Fred to come along, but she had soon realized that Fred would not allow it. He got a spare key for the hall, and she kept the apartment door open. She was stuck in the apartment, but she knew she wouldn't get a moment's sleep before they returned.

# Chapter 33

He stopped the car a few hundred yards from Kayne, killing the lights but not the engine. In the glove compartment, he found a pair of gloves and a ski mask. It annoyed him, no; it made him angry how a few tiny details could derail such a perfectly executed plan. The fire at Jack's was labeled an accident. When he had to take out Frank as well, of course, that would raise suspicions back to the Jack fire as well, but framing Carl for them both was easy enough. Now Carl was in prison and he couldn't frame him anymore. If only the cops hadn't been so quick to jump to their conclusions. The worst part was that he should have known that a fair part of Frank's possessions might still be at the store. After all, he hardly had any storage at the cabin.

He pulled the ski mask over his head and adjusted the hole for the eyes, so they only revealed the eyes, put the car in drive and put on his gloves as the car was slowly moving into Kayne. He was too deep into it now to back away. These were the last two pieces that needed to be taken care of. This time around, it was harder. An accident was out of the question; deliberately framing someone could easily backfire. He no longer cared who got framed for this, as long as it wasn't him. The alibi he had provided for himself was brilliant. Inspired by the Meadowses' trip to Spokane, that also gave him a brilliant opportunity; he had made himself an excuse to leave town and booked himself into a motel. After nightfall, he had snuck out of the motel through the back window and headed for a hidden rental he had rented under a false identity. The motel's security cameras would confirm that his car was there all night long.

The main street was all dark. The car drove almost to the end, where it turned and headed back before it stopped a few houses before the Salvation Army. This way, the car pointed in the right direction for his getaway. A quick look out on the street and the surrounding houses. All quiet. He pulled a key chain out of his pocket, having three keys in different colors. He needed the blue one first. The priority of his tasks was easy. As soon as the fire started, he needed to get away fast. That meant he needed to deal with the nosy lieutenant first. He stepped out of his car and walked determinedly toward the Salvation Army. The blue key slotted in place and he slowly turned it to not make too much of a sound. The door handle was carefully turned before the door opened and he was inside, changing from blue to yellow key. He climbed the stairs as he did the last time around, with one foot on each side. At the top of the stairs, the yellow key slotted in place and he turned it slowly. But there was no resistance and there came no clicking sound. The door was already open. It was not a kind of door that needed to be closed; after all, it wasn't a door leading out to the street. It only led out to the Army hall. Still, the last time, it had been locked at these hours. Maybe she was inconsistent or maybe she hadn't gone to bed yet. Or just because it was Saturday.

There had been no visible lights in the apartment. He opened the door carefully just enough so he could slip inside. He could see the lights from underneath the bathroom door. Maybe she was in the bathroom making herself ready for bed. He was about to move over to the bathroom door so he could wait for her as she got out when he saw the silhouette of a person sitting in the living room. He couldn't figure out why she was sitting in the dark, but it was the worst possible place. He had to cross maybe five yards before he could reach her. She could scream. She'd get time to put up a fight. However futile, it could be a lot more messy than he cared for. He pulled his knife. As soon as she moved, he would be ready for her.

Josie looked at her watch. It was two o'clock in the morning. It had been two desperate long hours. What if there came no arsonist, then they would sit there until the sun came up. That would be a long wait. She hoped the arsonist showed up, and that they caught him soon. She remembered the awkward silence during supper and couldn't quite imagine how it would be during breakfast if no one showed up. It would also be tough to explain to Lissie and Jonathan. At the same time, she felt bad about hoping someone would come to burn down her neighbor's house. Still, she could justify that a lot easier. Carl needed justice, Kayne needed justice too.

She was hungry. Well, not really. She was bored. But she figured something to eat would at least pass the time. She got up and headed to the kitchen. She opened the fridge. It was fuller than ever. She had brought in quite a lot of food for the two meals she had promised Fred and his friends. Mostly bought out of guilt. But she couldn't eat it all. She had to save something for that impressive breakfast she had promised them in the morning. But there had to be something she could make. It seemed she had plenty of time on her hands.

When he saw the figure getting up, he clutched his knife even harder. He watched the figure move toward the kitchen, and as soon as she disappeared into the kitchen, he moved into the living room. A small light went on in the kitchen. Coming closer, he saw her standing, staring into the fridge. The light in the kitchen was the light from the fridge. He had to restrain himself from moving too fast. He hoped she used long enough to decide for him to sneak up on her unnoticed. With the knife first, he snuck through the kitchen door. It was a tiny kitchen, and he was just a few yards off to planting the knife into her back. Just a few more steps, he lifted the knife for the stab and the shiny blade made a tiny glimmer in the light from the fridge.

# Chapter 34

The tiny glimmer warned Josie. She turned and saw a dark figure with a knife before her. Instinctively, she threw what she could get her hands on in the direction of the person with the knife. *I need Fred*, was her only thought. She took a kitchen chair and crashed it into the kitchen window, making it burst into a thousand pieces.

"Help, help me!" she screamed out before she threw the chair at the perpetrator.

A glass bowl containing some wet, meaty stuff came at him. Instinctively, he tried to catch it, and in the process, he lost his knife. He fumbled after the knife. The gloves made it tricky. He heard the glass break and Josie crying for help. Good luck with that, he thought, and grasped around his knife. He looked up and managed just to fend off a chair that came flying toward him.

"Help me!" she cried once more, but now he was on her. He laid his left hand hard over her mouth, preventing her from screaming any more, and stabbed hard toward her chest. She barely held back the knife. He might be older, but he was stronger and heavier than her. He leaned on her, using his body weight over his arm and pressing it down inch by inch.

The sound of breaking glass had woken the police officers up from the haze that one naturally comes into when you're tired and stare at a monitor or blank out in the air for hours. But all of a sudden, they were wide awake. They heard someone screaming but couldn't quite figure out what or where from. The second time, they heard it clearer.

# LIKE SMOKE IN THE WIND

"It's Josie," Fred said, and dropped all he had in his hands. "Come on." He was already on his way, and the other two followed as soon as they could get on their feet.

"Josie, I'm coming," he shouted into the night.

The other police officers caught up with him as he struggled with the keys in the main door.

"Stay behind Harry," he shouted as he pulled the door open and ran up toward the stairs. The doors into the apartment were open. He ran into the living room and stood for a few seconds to orientate himself. Then he saw the tiny light from the kitchen and heard a weak moaning sound. He ran into the kitchen and found Josie on the floor, holding one hand on her chest.

"Are you hurt?" he cried out.

"A little, I think," she replied.

"Can I take a look?" he said and slowly removed her hand. Josie nodded.

"Find me a towel, Don."

Don searched through the drawers of the kitchen, while Fred looked at the wound. It was a big red circle of blood on her T-shirt. He tore the shirt and revealed the wound. Don handed him a towel, and he started wiping blood.

"It doesn't look like it came beneath the ribs. I believe you'll be okay," Fred said and sighed in relief.

He heard a male voice responding to Josie's call for help, and he realized he'd be trapped in the house. The apartment had only one way in and out of it, and that was the narrow stairway from the hall. He had no choice but to leave. He saw there was blood on the knife. With the long waiting time for an ambulance in these parts, he hoped it would be enough. Frank's papers had to be dealt with later. Now he needed to get out. He had heard someone at the door as he came down the stairs and had just reached to hide inside the kitchen before the police officers came charging through the door and up the stairs. He had been lucky, after all. It seemed there had been some sort of surveillance he almost walked straight into. His biggest problem now was the police officer left behind. The police officer faced the main door and stood with his back to him, only a few feet away. He grabbed a skillet and slowly opened the kitchen door.

He wouldn't repeat his mistake of going too slow. This time, he was over him in a second and slammed the skillet in the back of his head. The police officer went down and the coast was clear.

"Did you hear that?" Don said. There was a slight muted thump and an 'ouch' coming from downstairs.

"Harry," Fred said, and both men were on their way. Don arrived first and knelt down beside Harry. Beside him on the floor lay the skillet the assailant had hit him with.

"Harry, how are you?" he said as he turned him around.

"Ah, my head hurts so bad," he stuttered. His eyes were almost closed as if the light was too bright, while in fact, it was almost dark in the room.

"He's had a concussion," Fred said as he looked at him.

Harry pointed toward the door.

"Away, he got away," he whispered. Fred got up and ran out to check, only to see the taillights of a car being turned on far down the road.

"Sure, he got away."

"How is he?" Josie came down the stairs, still wearing the bloody, torn T-shirt, and clutching the towel on the stab wound. "There's a doctor in Ashville. Should I call him?"

"I think that's for the best," Fred said. "Do you have somewhere to lay him down?"

"There's a bed in my guest room, but it's upstairs, I'm afraid."

"No problem, I can walk," Harry insisted. Don supported him up the stairs and Josie showed him the bed before she called for the doctor.

"Did you recognize your assailant?" Fred asked. They all sat in the dark guest room with only a tiny bit of light streaming in from the living room. None of them felt it was right to leave him alone.

"No, he was all covered up."

"But his voice?"

"He never spoke."

"You say he? Are you certain it was a man?" Don broke in.

"No, but it was a masculine body."

## LIKE SMOKE IN THE WIND

"I guess at least some of your theories must have something right, since someone thought you needed to be put away."

Josie told them about all she had discovered and all of her theories. She was still talking when the doctor came. The local ambulance came right behind.

"From the looks of it, it's a severe concussion. I think it's best to send him to a hospital for a more thorough check."

Harry insisted he could walk and got angry when the paramedics suggested a stretcher, but they got him into the ambulance and drove away to Spokane. Fred sent Don with the doctor to Ashville to pick up the car, while he went to get all the gear they had left behind.

"Can't make out the plates on the car, and I'm afraid that's all we have to go on," Fred said, playing the tape of the car going up and down the main street.

"What car is it?"

"A Ford Fiesta or something, quite a compact car."

"No one in Kayne has such a small car. I've got the smallest car in Kayne. And I believe they all swear to a Detroit-made V8 of some kind," Josie said. "But an outsider doesn't make sense. Could someone have hired a hit man?"

"No offense, but if he had been professional, you'd be dead by now."

Josie nodded. She realized that someone who made a living by killing would be more effective with his knife. She realized that in her misfortune, she'd been quite lucky.

"Wait a minute." Josie found her laptop and started a search. "It could be a rental. There's a lot of Fiestas leased out by rental companies."

"Of course, but unless we can find out exactly what car it was and link it to the assailant, then it just won't stick." Fred got up from his chair and walked around the living room in circles. "I fear we're back to square one."

"Square one what?" Don arrived in the doorway.

"We don't have any leads at all on either the fires or the attack on Josie and Harry."

"But the cameras?" Don asked.

"Sorry, nothing but a small Ford Fiesta."

"So now we need to tell the sheriff that we need to reopen a closed investigation but with no good leads.?"

"Yup," Fred said. He sat down by the table and supported his head on his hands as if the new worries weighed it down.

"So now what?"

"We start from scratch, but it won't be easy. He is clever and has hidden his tracks well so far."

"I'm sorry, I shouldn't have done this," Josie said.

"Don't beat yourself up; you were right and you did what you had to do to get our attention." Josie wasn't sure if Fred really meant it or if was just being nice because she almost got killed.

"The most important thing is that you're okay," Don said.

"One of you can take the guest room, and if the other cares to crash on the couch, I will make that superb late breakfast for you." Josie looked at her watch. It was past four in the morning.

"And tomorrow, if you would humor me just one last time."

"One more time for what?"

"To make a last house call. I know how to find the rental."

# Chapter 35

Breakfast had been well after noon and the mood had been lighter after some hours of sleep and some food. Fred had been on the phone with Harry. He had been lucky; it was a concussion, but he'd be all right. They needed to wait a couple of hours for the house call. It was already getting dim outside when Josie walked through the cold empty streets of Kayne with two cops on a Sunday afternoon. The gravel up the long driveway to George's house crackled under their feet, telling them the ground wasn't frozen yet.

"This was a nice surprise, Lieutenant, and is this the young police officer that's with you?" George acted surprised by seeing Fred and Don, even though she told him on the phone that she was bringing Fred and a colleague. George probably thought the reason was that there was some truth to the rumors after all. The ones stating that there was something going on between Josie and the police inspector. And that for some reason, they wanted to announce it to him first.

"Come on in. I've made you some tea. I don't know about the inspectors, what they drink."

"They're as pitiful as the rest of you lot," she said as she stepped in and unbuttoned her coat. "So they drink coffee."

George showed them into the living room and Josie went over and greeted Jerry and Oscar, who each sat in their chair around the coffee table. George had set the table for them to sit on the couch, but Josie showed the police officers to the dining table in the background, and took a third chair, and placed it halfway between the dining and the coffee table. She was about to sit down, but changed her mind and decided to stand. The informal setting George had invited them into was suddenly very formal.

"I need to talk to you about something important. I need to give you some information about Deirdre; your daughter," she said and nodded toward George, "your sister, and your cousin," she said, looking at Jerry and Oscar respectively. "It's now only fifteen days since I first heard the name Deirdre

Chisholm, when Jack mentioned it at the flea market. And a lot of things have happened here since then."

"It was a tragedy. We just don't like talking about it, that's all," Oscar broke in.

"Jack said something about a secret that he had kept for her. And I suspected this secret could be the key to solve this petty fight between you, George, and Frank. Even though I'm too late to do anything about that, I kept looking into it."

"Doesn't matter; nothing you ever could have said would have evened the matters with that cheap liar," George said with his fist trembling in the air. Josie was glad she had the police officers behind her, or she guessed they would have thrown her out. At least now he knew she wasn't there to show off a potential boyfriend.

"Maybe my information at least can bring you some kind of closure," she said.

"What's that about a secret anyway? Deirdre never kept any secrets from me," George said. Josie couldn't help smiling at the idea that the old man still believed that an eighteen-year-old daughter told her daddy everything. She forced the smile away. It really wasn't the time. Nobody asked what the secret she had found out was, but she answered as if they had asked.

"I'm not entirely sure what the secret was, but it could be that she withdrew her application to the Salvation Army training college."

"What?" Jerry and George uttered almost simultaneously. The disbelief was written on both of their faces.

"She would never do that," Jerry continued. "It was all she ever talked about."

"She would certainly have told me," George broke in.

"I have read the letter she sent to DHQ. I can arrange it so that you get a copy if you'd like."

George looked straight out in the air and struggled to control his breath.

"Or maybe it was the reason for her withdrawal," Josie continued as if nothing had happened.

"And that was?" Jerry asked.

"She was pregnant."

## LIKE SMOKE IN THE WIND

This time, neither George, Jerry, nor Oscar said anything. They just looked at Josie with platter-round eyes.

"And this you know for sure?" George said in an accusing tone.

"I'm sorry this was never conveyed to you in a proper manner a long time ago, but the police report clearly states that she was pregnant," Fred said, and drew the hostile looks away from Josie for a moment.

"Who's the father? Was it Jack? That..."

"That's not a bad guess. She liked Jack a lot, but she gave up on him. She chose to be an officer still. And as you said, she wouldn't risk that for anything."

"That doesn't make any sense," Jerry broke in. "If she wouldn't do anything that could risk her plans, how did she become pregnant?"

"That is the third secret. How did she become pregnant?"

The tension in the room scaled off the charts. Josie walked slowly back to the dining table and leaned herself against it, as she needed some kind of support.

"She was raped," she said with all the calm she could muster. "In this very house and in her own bed. And by her own cousin."

"What!" Oscar exclaimed. "That's outrageous, coming here with accusations like that; that's just not possible."

"I can even tell you the exact date. On March eleventh, nineteen seventy-eight. You had been out with a girl, but she wouldn't sleep with you, so you forced yourself on her. But she got away before you could fulfill the rape."

"So what, it's too old, statute of limitations, you know," Oscar objected.

"That's true, it's way too old," Fred broke in.

"Then you went home, and you raped Deirdre."

"How can you know that?" George said.

"It was the day after she talked to you about sending Oscar away. The smoking was just an excuse. By that time, the Salvation Army rules against smoking only applied to officers and certain under officers. She had no reason to react more than you on this matter. Later in the Sunday meeting, Oscar looked at her and laughed. That caused Deirdre to miss the notes on the piano for the only time anyone can remember." Josie had checked up on when Jonathan's sister became a soldier. It had been the following day. "It was the time of conception. Deirdre was clearly out of balance and you, Oscar, were the one that caused it."

"That still proves nothing."

"If you want proof, the child is buried along with Deirdre. We can still pull DNA and test for parenthood," Fred broke in. It was a half bluff because he wasn't sure if tissue still had survived after all these years.

"Well, but I didn't kill her." Oscar got up from the chair and shouted at Josie.

"You really did it," George said, his voice was thin as a whisper. "You raped my girl. We gave you a home. I cared for you as a son, and you did this to me?" George's voice ran out of air and tears flooded down his cheek. Josie felt an urge to get over and hold the old man as he was crying louder and louder. But right now, she couldn't. Jerry did. He went over to his father and held him.

"I don't have to be here," Oscar said and stormed out. Don was on his feet, but Josie held up her hand and signaled him to let him go.

# Chapter 36

"Oscar didn't kill her. He got that one right," she said after Oscar had slammed the door shut on his way out. Once again, she had the attention of everyone in the room.

"I know he didn't. That was an accident," George said. "But an accident that shouldn't have happened if Frank had done his job as he promised."

Josie reached into her bag and pulled out the old lock from Jack's nightstand.

"This is one of only two things that were rescued from the fire at Jack's," she said, and placed the lock on the coffee table in front of George and Jerry. "This is the lock Frank ordered to go into the old mill."

"It's a little late now, isn't it?" Jerry replied.

Josie said nothing, just went to her bag and found a folding knife and a flat screwdriver. Then she went over to the desk in the corner and took the frame with all the keys down and placed it on the desk.

"Sorry about this," she said as she took the knife and placed the blade into the crackled line around the frame and yanked up a corner of the glass, then by using the knife and the screwdriver, prying it out inch by inch. "One of these keys always puzzled me because it was out of place," she said and took the key in the second row that was longer than the others in the row. "I'm sorry it took me so long to figure out why." She brought the key over to the coffee table and took the lock. It was already in the locked position. She put the key in the lock and turned it around. With a gentle click, it returned to the open position. "How would you like to explain why you have the key for a lock that was in Jack's possession?"

"Those keys fit a lot of locks," George argued.

"Not quite so," Josie objected, and held up the lock. "This lock was custom made to replace a hundred-year-old lock, but still had modern safety features. This is a rare lock, and very few, if any, other keys fit into it."

## ISAAC LIND

Fred got up from his chair and took the lock away from Josie and examined it. "It would be an easy task to find out if this key belongs to this actual lock," he commented. Then he placed the lock and key on the table in front of him on the dining table, making sure any evidence was in police hands.

"There's one more piece to the puzzle," Josie said and found her bag and pulled the old receipt out of it. "Why was Frank murdered and why did his house need to be burnt to the ground?" Josie pulled the chair she had abandoned on the middle of the living room floor and pulled it over to the coffee table and sat down facing George and Jerry. "This explains why the key for the lock ordered specifically for the mill ended up in your possession, the very paper proof Frank talked about."

Both men sat in silence, neither of them sure what they were looking at. Josie handed the receipt to Fred, who got up from his chair and took it.

"It's a receipt for 'changing the lock at the Kayne Mill, and for receiving the key' and," Fred said with a dramatic pause. "It's signed by G. Chisholm."

"That's a lie. It's a falsification," George exclaimed. He was on the verge of getting up, sitting on the edge of the sofa, pointing at Fred and the receipt. His face was red as burning coal and Josie for a minute worried that his poor heart would finally give in. "I never signed such a receipt."

This time, Jerry didn't move in to comfort his father. Josie reached over the coffee table and put her hand on George's shoulder and looked him straight in his eyes. "No, George, you didn't."

The old man calmed down. Fred, however, looked down at the receipt, puzzled. What they believed to be a vital part of evidence, and it wasn't after all.

"So who could sign the receipt in your name in a town where everyone knew each other?" Fred asked.

"Frank did it to smear me," George said.

"But that doesn't explain how the key ended up here in your living room," Josie said. "No, it was indeed signed by a G. Chisholm, but not George – it was signed by Jerry, or Gerald, as is your given name."

"But he was only a kid back then. He couldn't be more than thirteen, fourteen years old. How could they let him sign out the key?" Fred objected this time.

"Because Kayne is a small town where everyone knows each other, and it was just a key for a mill that wasn't in use. Jerry probably ran errands for George all the time," she said. George nodded, while Jerry sat in silence. "So Jerry thinks he could just hold on to it a couple of weeks. No one would know, and he could use the mill as his private clubhouse."

Josie shifted her weight on the chair and leaned back. "And here is where it all comes together. Deirdre is pregnant. She has already sent the withdrawal letter to the Salvation Army. But there are a few things she needs to fix before she can break the news to her father." Josie paused slightly and looked straight at George. "I believe you are right. It troubled her to keep secrets from you. Still, it was this one thing she needed to fix. The kid needed a father, and we all know that the real father was not an option. I guess we all know that Jack was the best option she could think of. I believe he would gladly accept fatherhood to get the chance of marrying the love of his life. So she tells him, or hands him a note or something and asks him to meet up by the old mill, which had become a quiet place since it was closed down."

*Kayne April 1978*

She stepped out of the door. It was getting dark, but the spring was on its way and it was a calm evening. It was early; she knew. She regretted telling him to meet so late in the evening. The entire afternoon, she had anxiously wandered around, waiting for the clock to move on. All the time, she had rehearsed her speech. Then she had put on makeup. She knew he liked her. He had told her, and even if he hadn't, it was easy enough to notice. But she wanted to look good. This wasn't just plan A, it was the only plan. There were other boys that liked her, but Jack was the one she wanted to be with. But with nothing left to do, she slipped out of the house as early as quarter past eight. It would give her a long wait at the mill, but the walls drove her crazy at the moment. She walked up Silver Lake Road and hoped no one would notice her. Looking down on the blacktop and walking as casually as possible, as if that would make any kind of difference. If anyone came down this way, they were bound to notice her. But she met no one and sighed with relief when she passed Hunter's Road and knew she had passed the last houses on her way. Now she could sit on the grass outside the mill and watch the setting sun and just wait until Jack showed up. She went up behind the mill and jumped over the river on the back, where it was narrow, and got over to the opposite side of the mill. She sat down on the grass and watched the thin red line as the sun set on the horizon. She replayed the conversation with Jack once more in her head, like she had done numerous times this afternoon. Sometimes she imagined he said no and left. Other times, she imagined a yes. Those times made her uncertain. What happened next? Would she kiss him? Or would he kiss her? The thought made her giddy inside. Being with Jack would be a good consolation when she couldn't become an officer. It would be worse if he turned her down.

She sat there about five minutes before she heard a noise inside the mill. She became furious that despite her father's strict banning use of the mill, someone still used it. And she was in a desperate need to get them away so that she could talk to Jack in private. She tried to get back to the front of the mill without making a sound, eager to catch them in the act. The planks that Frank and her father had nailed in front of the door were gone and she found the door unlocked. She heard low voices inside and could smell cigarettes. She stepped inside and a rush of wind suddenly slammed the door shut. There were some movements inside the mill. They probably realized that someone came. She ran through the first corridor. They heard her, and she could hear them giggle as they ran out through the other corridor.

"Jerry, is that you?" she shouted and ran after them. She noticed the back of Jerry leaving out the door as she rounded the corner. She ran over to the door, but as soon as she reached the door, the lock gave a clicking sound and it was shut.

"Jerry, you come back here at once, or I'll make sure you'll regret it," she shouted and shook the door handle as hard as she could, but the door was solid and hardly moved. She shouted even louder. "Jerry!"

She stopped and listened. It was all quiet. Had he just gone away? She looked at her watch. Jack would be here in half an hour. If she hadn't made it out by then, he would certainly help her. She looked around after some kind of tools that she could use to open the door. Nothing. She kicked the door and slammed it with both hands.

"Help!" she screamed once again. Nothing, not a sound.

## LIKE SMOKE IN THE WIND

"You know this story," Josie said and looked at Jerry. "You just dropped the cigarettes down and ran off." She looked from Jerry and to George. "How long she was by the door screaming for help and trying to get out, I don't know, but when she realized the fire was in the other room, it was too late to do anything about it."

Josie paused and all they could hear was George's heavy breathing. Father and son didn't look at each other. They both stared down at the table. Josie inhaled slowly and braced herself.

# Chapter 37

"Finally, of course, Jack came along. But by then, the mill was in full flames," Josie said before she continued laying out her theory.

*Kayne April 1978*

Deirdre had been so secretive when she had asked him to meet her at the mill at nine o'clock this evening. She had given him a smile that puzzled him. It felt so... so flirty. She had always been nice to him, but also always clear on the fact that it couldn't be anything between them because she was going to be an officer in the Salvation Army. That meant that she could only marry another officer in the Salvation Army. Jack had even considered it, but had to realize that he wasn't cut out for those things. But now he was puzzled. She had never asked him anything of this sort before. He had combed through his hair and put on a clean shirt. Now, suddenly, he feared it would make him look silly. What if he had read too much into the situation? It was possible that he had. He curled up his newly ironed shirt in his hands to look more casual. He was nervous, and the nerves added on as he walked up the road.

In retrospect, he couldn't remember if it was the sound of burning wood or the smell of the thick smoke that caught his attention first and made him look up. As he saw the mill in full flames, his first thought was that she could be inside. After all, he knew they had the key. He ran as fast as he could up the hill.

"Deirdre," he shouted as he reached the mill.

"Jack," she replied. The voice came from inside the mill. He ran to the door, but it was locked.

"I can't open the door," she replied.

"But the key, don't you have the key?" he replied.

"There is no key."

## LIKE SMOKE IN THE WIND

Jack was about to argue with her, but he suddenly realized what the situation was. He could run to the Chisholms, hope to find the key, but he couldn't make himself leave her.

"Wait, I'll get you out." He threw himself toward the door, but it was useless. The door was too solid. He searched around the mill and found an old shovel. He slammed the shovel repeatedly against the door like an axe. The marks on the door were tiny. He hit it around the lock. The door was thinner there because of the carved out slot for the lock. Still, it wasn't easy. It was an oak door set in with linseed oil and the wood was hard as rock.

"Hold on, Deirdre, just hold on," he shouted as he hit the door as hard as he could.

For ten whole minutes, he pounded on the door and was drenched in sweat when the door finally gave in. He found Deirdre on the floor, just inside the door. He reached under her arms and pulled her out, far from the fire and into breathable air.

"Deirdre, speak to me," he said and shook her shoulders. She opened her eyes and forced a tiny smile. Jack smiled back. She wiped soot away from his face and whispered. Jack leaned in to hear what she was saying.

"I was going to ask you..." She stopped and breathed. "To marry me."

"Of course I will," Jack said and smiled. "There's nothing else in the world I'd rather do."

"I'm afraid it's too late now," she whispered.

"Don't say that. Hang in there, Deirdre." Jack said, but he could see she was too weak. "But I changed the lock. How could this happen? I gave the key to Jerry..." He paused as the last pieces of the puzzles were laid. "Did Jerry do this?"

Deirdre drew her breath and tried to speak, but nothing came out. She gathered all her force and drew her breath deep enough the utter a few words.

"Promise me."

"Promise you what?" Jack said.

He could really see her struggle to draw her breath, and somehow he knew that this would be her last.

"No one must know about Je..." Her head fell to the side and the life that always had sparkled in her eyes faded out.

"I promise," Jack said repeatedly, and he clutched her in his arms. He had no concept of how long he sat there before others arrived. The first one arriving at the scene just checked that she was dead and they let him sit there holding Deirdre. When George came, he had to let her go. It was as his whole life was ripped into pieces when she was pulled away from him.

"Before the fire ruin was investigated, Jack found the old lock. He burned it and managed to lock it before he replaced it with the one on the scene. That is why the police found a hundred-year-old malfunctioning lock on the scene. The new lock, he kept in his nightstand."

Josie got up from the chair and put it back on the dining table. "You must have known that Jack knew. He was the one who signed out the key to you, and the last one to see Deirdre."

"Of course I knew; he told me. He said he wouldn't tell, because he promised Deirdre," Jerry said. "Worked fine for me, but then he got demented and I could no longer trust him."

"He was just a kid and, after all, the fire was an accident," George objected.

"Sure, if you had come forward back then, Jerry. But you didn't. Did you?" Josie leaned forward and looked Jerry deep into his eyes. "And for every year you walked around with that secret, it got harder and harder to tell the truth. I believe the lies consumed you, and when Jack threatened to expose you, coming out clean wasn't an option. So you killed him to preserve the lie."

Jerry looked at her like a smug card player with an ace up his sleeve, still to be revealed, but he said nothing.

"Then, Frank started talking about his infamous piece of paper, and you knew what it was, so you killed him too. When you realized that the paper most likely was stored in the hardware store, you came last night to burn it down. What I didn't guess was that you would try to kill me and assault a police officer as well."

"Are you done?" Jerry asked with a nonchalant air of confidence.

"Pretty much," Josie said.

"Good luck proving that, Lieutenant," he said and his smile broadened. "I was on a business trip to Spokane. I stayed at the Hill Ridge Motel."

"Excuse me, where did you stay?" Fred broke in. He had been texting on his phone and just momentarily looked up.

# LIKE SMOKE IN THE WIND

"Hill Ridge Motel," Jerry repeated. "And if you check, I'm sure the security cameras can verify that my car stayed there all night."

"Sure, we will," Fred mumbled.

"Do you have anything more to add? Running around spreading false accusations. Not very Christian of you, Lieutenant."

"I do have more. You parked the car probably right in front of the cameras, so you were certain it would be taped. And then you rented a car from a car rental business in a walking distance from the motel so at night you could sneak out of the motel and drive the rental back to Kayne while your car gave you your alibi."

"That's insane," Jerry said. He was still calm, but his demeanor was not as smug as earlier.

"I can take it from here if you please, Josie."

"Sure," she said and moved to the back as Fred got up.

"It's your hassle to give yourself an alibi that actually frames you. I have some colleagues on their way to pick up the car as we speak." Fred moved toward the chair Josie placed in front of the Chisholms and leaned on the top rail. "They have a picture of you to show the clerk that handled the lease, and even if you signed with a false identity, we can compare handwriting. We filmed the car as it entered and left Kayne last night."

Jerry had lost his calm, and drops of sweat ran down his forehead.

"So you killed them all?" George said with terror in his eyes.

"I had to. I realized that she wasn't going to let it rest, and sooner or later, it would all surface."

Fred placed the chair back at the dining table and stepped up in front of the Chisholms. Don got up right behind him.

"Gerald Chisholm, I'm placing you under arrest for the murder on Deirdre Chisholm, Jack Sutton and Frank Meadows, and for the attempted murder on Josie Facundo, and assault on a police officer."

Jerry calmly got up and moved around the table and placed himself in front of Fred.

"I beat you twice, but I should have understood that the stupid receipt would still be at the store." He stopped as Don came over and cuffed him. "If it hadn't been for that, you'd never have caught me."

175

## ISAAC LIND

Fred looked at him without the least interest in Jerry's little speech. He just read him his Miranda rights. Jerry looked at Josie, who had withdrawn slightly to let the police officers do their job.

"If you hadn't been so nosy, Jack and Frank might still be alive today."

"No," Fred objected. "If you hadn't killed them, then they surely would have still been alive today."

Fred took hold of Jerry's left arm and Don the other, and they led him out.

"So many, how could you, Jerry?" George said as Jerry was walked out between the police officers. Jerry didn't answer.

Moments later, the door was shut, and Josie was left with George.

"I can't believe what makes a man do such a thing. The first one I know wasn't deliberate, but the others he planned for the smallest detail. How could my son turn into such a monster?"

"He was carrying a huge sin for all those years. It will eventually eat you up inside."

"I guess you're right."

George rested his head in his hands.

"I am truly sorry for bringing you such bad news." Josie moved slowly toward him and sat down in a chair next to where he sat.

"Well, I'm not going to shoot the messenger," he replied. George took a deep breath before he exhaled. The old man that always looked so vibrant and young compared to his actual age now looked like he had aged a decade during one evening.

"I prefer the hard truth over a sweetened lie," Josie said.

George nodded. "You're right, and one day, I will appreciate this."

For a man who'd effectively lost his whole family in one blow, he was taking it well. But that was what George Chisholm was all about; keeping appearances whatever happened. Still, in his eyes, one could see the beaten man.

"I'm sorry I couldn't tell you this while Frank was still alive," she said after a moment's silence. George's face broke up and the dam breached, releasing a flood of tears down his cheeks.

"He was my best friend," he stuttered out. "My best friend and I hated him for forty years for something that wasn't his fault."

Josie nodded and decided on saying as little as possible.

"I truly hated my friend."

# LIKE SMOKE IN THE WIND

He tried in vain to wipe the tears with his hands.

"Excuse me," he said and got up and into the kitchen. He turned on the water, but she could still hear him sobbing. Josie sat there waiting for several minutes. At one point, she wondered if she should leave, but that felt awkward as well. Finally, he got back. He looked a lot fresher, and his face was still moist from being washed.

"You know you have a last chance to pay Frank the respect he deserves," she said.

"I guess you're right. It's the least I can do."

"And there is still someone you can apologize to."

"But..."

"No one can undo what's done. Now you just need to make the right choices and take the right path."

George nodded.

"Frank's funeral is on Wednesday. I expect to see you there."

# Chapter 38

The day was damp, foggy, and gray. No rain, just a thick fog covering the cemetery. It was one of these days that would dampen your mood and give you a headache. This day couldn't be dampened any more. Almost the entire population of Kayne was dressed in black and cramped together in the graveyard.

As the last verse of the final hymn was sung by rusty old voices, the fog cleared just enough to let a little ray of sunshine through all the gray. People's faces lit up with smiles, as if they all understood that the light streaming through the clouds was actually a thumbs-up from the Lord. A 'don't you worry, I've got it covered up here. Frank is all good.' For Josie, this was easier than last week. Frank had family, and they could take care of each other. Not like Carl, who had no one else except the one that was buried. Josie felt a responsibility for him the whole day. Now, after the final amen, Josie offered her condolences to the Meadows family. When that was done, she could smoothly ease away and her job was done for this time. She sneaked off to a bystander a bit by himself.

"Nice of you to come, Inspector," she said.

"It's a bit special," Fred replied. "It's my first murder case."

They stood there looked at all the people paying their respects. Carl was out of prison and using his second-hand suit for the second time, paying his respects to someone he didn't like during life. But today, he wasn't the person in need; now he was the one offering the condolences.

"I probably wouldn't get this investigation if we'd realized it was a murder right away."

"Too young?" Josie said and pondered the bizarre idea that a murder probably was good for the career.

"Way too young. Many inspectors go through their entire career without conducting a murder investigation, and I got a triple murderer before turning thirty."

## LIKE SMOKE IN THE WIND

They looked at Carl walking away with a smile on his face. He was out of prison, cleared from all charges, and at least in times of grief, they accepted him into the community. Josie only hoped it would last.

"But I owe you big time, Josie. I could easily have ended up with the wrong guy."

"But you didn't. You did the right thing when it was called for," Josie said.

"I probably wouldn't figure it out without you."

"Maybe I'll call in that favor one day," she said. "By the way, how's Harry doing?"

"He's fine. It was a light concussion. He was released from the hospital on Monday."

The crowd spread out as people who had paid their respects were leaving. The line with people still waiting to say some words of comfort and shake a hand or give a hug was getting shorter. At the very end of the line was a man that had been an old man as long as Josie had known him, but it had never been as visible as right now. George looked like he carried the burdens of the entire world on his shoulders. He attended the funeral that he, for years, had sworn he wouldn't go to, but now he had to force himself to go, knowing that the pain they were in was inflicted by his family.

He had tried as long as possible to stay on the gravel, but the last bit of the grave was out on the grass, and it was dripping wet. The black leather shoes were old, and the sole was thin, and before he reached them, he could feel his feet getting wet. It was stupid having such old shoes when he could perfectly well afford some new ones. But he liked these. He had grown used to them. It went to show how stubborn he really was. So much he could have avoided if it wasn't for this stupid stubbornness. He cursed his wet shoes and promised that he would buy some new ones. Albeit, not in Ashville. The old shoe-shop in Ashville where he had bought these had closed down a decade ago, and he didn't like the new one that had opened instead. *There's bound to be a decent shop in Spokane,* he thought. He had stopped some feet away from the mourning family and hadn't noticed that he was the next in line.

"George," Jonathan Meadows said. George looked up and was taken by surprise.

"Words," he stuttered with a swelling throat. "I can't seem to find any words." His eyes were filled up with tears that rolled down his face as he stretched out a weak and trembling hand. "I'm afraid there are none."

Jonathan shook his hand and pulled him in and gave him a friendly bear hug.

"I don't need any words; your outstretched hand is enough, and I know Dad would have taken it as well."

"You think?" The old man was shaking in the arms of Jonathan.

"I know," he replied. "If Dad sees us now, he is smiling."

Lissie came over and hugged him as well. After a short spell, his sisters came over and just patted him on his shoulders. Their husbands stood a bit apart and looked slightly uneasy. They had heard the story about the old arch enemies, but not the story about the two best friends that once were pillars in the tiny community.

The shimmer of sunlight had grown, and the sun was about to conquer the thick fog. As the old man left the Meadowses alone, there were only small cottony clouds of fog left. And with the sun shining on his face, he afforded himself a little smile as he greeted Josie and the inspector on his way back to the car park.

As the family followed the rest of the crowd back to the cars, Jonathan and Lissie went over to Josie and Fred.

"You were right, Lieutenant," he said. "It's always better knowing the right man is behind bars."

Josie just smiled as a reply.

"Thank you so much," Lissie added and gave them both a hug, and they followed the rest.

"So what's your next case, Lieutenant?" Fred asked as they were alone again.

"Probably something trivial, a homeless guy that has forgotten who he is or something."

"Good for that homeless guy, knowing he's got the best detective in the Salvation Army on the case, then," he said.

## LIKE SMOKE IN THE WIND

Josie smiled. She assumed he meant it as a compliment, even if it was an awkward one. She turned toward him and gave him a warm hug. "Can I rely on your help then too?"

"Always," he said as he patted her back. "But I see what you mean," Fred continued. "The truth needs to be revealed before the healing can begin."

The end

ISAAC LIND

For more info on the author visit my webpage:
https://isaac-lind.com

CPSIA information can be obtained
at www.ICGtesting.com
Printed in the USA
LVHW012050191122
733278LV00036B/1998